"It's hard to know what you're feeling in here, it's so dark."

A chuckle from deep in Ward's chest filled the elevator. "Oh, believe me, I know what I'm touching."

Pure desire raced through her. Hannah quickly returned to patting the floor. She needed that blouse now for more than the ruse of being chilled. She needed protection against the potent, sexual promise of Ward. And her own need to be very, very naughty.

Their fingers entwined as they found her blouse at the same time. He trailed his hand up her arm to rest at her shoulder. All his other touches had been accidents. But not this one.

Hannah couldn't move away. She hadn't purposely touched another person sexually in over four years. But here it was dark. Ward would never see her body. Never see what she had to hide. The dark had become her favorite companion, and now it would give her something else. A chance to feel, if only briefly, like a woman again.

Every function in her body stilled. Waited. Then Ward's lips covered hers.

Blaze™

Dear Reader,

Before I wrote *Share the Darkness*, I read a couple books where the heroine was afraid of the dark. Being a little bit contrary, I immediately began thinking about a heroine who preferred the dark—embraced it, even. Then along came the Harlequin Blaze Author Search Contest and I knew I had the perfect place to pitch my new idea. All I had to do was write the story....

So, armed with ten pages and synopsis, I entered—and received Honorable Mention. I still remember getting that phone call. I'd just placed the toddler in the high chair when the phone rang. Thank goodness for dry cereal!

I really wanted to write about a woman who'd made some questionable choices in her life…maybe gotten involved with the wrong man for the wrong reasons. So Hannah Garrett, a woman who's attracted to danger…and to dangerous men, was born.

I hope you enjoy reading about the independent woman she becomes as much as I enjoyed walking a little on the dark side!

I'd love to hear from you. E-mail me at jill@jillmonroebooks.com or visit my Web site at www.jillmonroebooks.com.

Happy reading!

Jill

Books by Jill Monroe

HARLEQUIN TEMPTATION
1003—NEVER NAUGHTY ENOUGH

SHARE THE DARKNESS

Jill Monroe

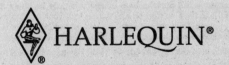

TORONTO • NEW YORK • LONDON
AMSTERDAM • PARIS • SYDNEY • HAMBURG
STOCKHOLM • ATHENS • TOKYO • MILAN • MADRID
PRAGUE • WARSAW • BUDAPEST • AUCKLAND

This book is dedicated to Jenn Stone and
Donnell Epperson—your continued good health is my greatest wish!

As always, I'd like to thank my family, for their endless encouragement and for
overlooking dust, stacks of paper and more fast-food meals than home-cooked ones.
I'll try to do better, Mom!

Special thanks to my editor, Jennifer Green,
whose ideas and suggestions are always spot-on. You rock!

Thanks also to Brenda Chin for giving *Share the Darkness* Honorable Mention in the
Harlequin Blaze contest and encouraging me to write past those first ten pages.

Thanks to Kimberly Whalen. May this be the first of many!

For my critique partners: Kassia Krozser, Gena Showalter, Linda Rooks,
Angi Platt and Beth Cornelison—thanks for the red ink.

And to Jennifer, Karen, Maggie, Traci, Sheila,
Amanda and Betty—I can't imagine better friends.

Go, Wet Noodle Posse!

ISBN 0-373-79249-2

SHARE THE DARKNESS

1

WARD CASSIDY could think of better uses for an ice cube.

Although the way Hannah Garrett rolled the ice along her skin to cool the slope of her gorgeous neck still topped his list. He sucked in a breath as a droplet of water slowly ran past the inviting underside of her chin and slid down her throat, weaving a path along her collarbone and disappearing into the tantalizing area below.

Tantalizing because he hadn't thought of much else other than Hannah or her breasts since he'd gotten this awful assignment in the hottest place next to hell.

He liked his ice cold, and his women hot. And Hannah would make an ice cube melt in Siberia. Now she was lifting up her red curly hair and rubbing the cube on the back of her neck. Next to hell? *He was in hell.* Why'd his office have to face the break room?

The multiline telephone on his desk beeped an annoying jingle. Why couldn't phones just ring? The electronic chimelike sound literally tap-danced on his nerves.

Just then Hannah put the ice cube in her mouth and sucked. Desire shot through him as his mind conjured up images of those generous lips of hers surrounding him. His knuckles tightened around the cool plastic phone handle. But nothing could chill his white-hot arousal.

The phone chimed again, and he almost flung the damn thing across his desk. Whoever was daring to interrupt his stint as voyeur could take a train ride to hell. Or right here next to him in Gallem. The heat was probably about the same. He took a deep breath. *Get it together.*

Ward Cassidy, federal officer of the law, turned his chair with slow deliberation away from the break room where Hannah was perfecting her "cooling off" techniques.

Instead he concentrated on the view outside his window. He centered on the grass, parched just as he was. The office air conditioner couldn't chug out enough cold air to contend with the heat. He was acting a fool. Hannah was just a woman trying not to sizzle in the offices of Protter and Lane Investment Banking. And here he was taking his frustrations out on a poor defenseless telephone.

He lifted the handle before the damn thing could ring a third time, just barely remembering to use his cover name. "Coleman here."

A few clicks echoed in the background, and he immediately went on alert.

"We're on a secure line."

"I'll shut the door." Ward stood and closed the door, welcoming the barrier. A lot of good it did, a huge picture window still gave him a prime view of the break room.

He picked up the phone again. Ward recognized the voice of his friend and former partner at the Bureau. A few years ago, his colleague, Brett Haynes, was one of the best field agents. Now he was permanently desked after choosing the wife and family route over adventure and danger. Poor guy.

Good. Another person he could take his frustra-tions out on.

Ward resisted his urge to laugh out loud. "Why wouldn't the line be secure? The security around here is so lax any ten-year-old with low speed Internet access could hack into this place."

Brett's chuckle was loud and clear. In disgust, Ward angled his chair away from the window. Still his eyes once again drifted back to the break room. He gritted his teeth. Hannah hadn't left. Neither had the ice cube.

Although a human resources memo to employees had given permission to wear shorts in the office during the heat wave, Hannah's legs remained encased in pants. She didn't have a problem leaving her arms bare, though. She now ran the ice cube up the gentle curve of her bicep, then down the soft skin of her…

He knew her skin would be soft. He imagined his lips following such a path. Starting at her wrist, tracing his tongue on the delicate skin of her forearm, stopping only long enough to lick her inner elbow before…

I'm losing my mind. "You gotta pull me from this assignment."

"Can't. You really pissed off the boss lady with that stunt you pulled on your last case."

His lips twitched into a slow smile. "The bad guys are in prison, aren't they?"

"I think it's more like how they got there. Dragging two prisoners who've been hiding in the swampland of Louisiana for two weeks through Director James's office is not the best method for career advancement."

"She said I could never bring in the big ones. I wanted to show her that I could, to look good for the boss."

"Ha. You looked worse than they did. Forget it. You'll be in Gallem until this case is put to bed. Which shouldn't take too long with your skills. Any rookie could nail it."

Damn, why did he have to put it that way? When he thought nail, he only thought of...

Hannah was blotting her skin with a paper towel. Rubbing the thin paper along the column of her throat. He almost growled. He almost shouted at her to stop.

"I expect we'll be hitting the eighteenth hole by the end of the week."

"You'd be surprised. I've been thrown a few curves," Ward said.

"You? Nah. Actually, the reason why I called was to let you know the field office is sending me there for a check."

"No wife? No kid?"

"Just you, me and a beer."

Ward angled back in his chair as he watched Hannah ball the paper towel and lob it toward the trash can. "Now, that's the best offer I've had in two weeks."

"The ladies of Gallem not lining up at your door? You must be losing your touch."

He spotted Hannah's slim, sexy form pass by the small window of his door. No friendly wave, no courtesy smile from one employee to another. Yeah, she didn't like him. For the first time today he felt a chill.

"Having a dry spell." The show was over. Ward sat straight in his chair, and checked out the employee files. "Is Grace hassling you about leaving? After all, that's why you took that desk job."

"It's just an overnighter, and I think she's actually looking forward to me being out of her hair for a bit."

"Great. Come by the office Saturday, and I'll introduce you to corporate hell." Ward replaced the receiver. He reached in his pocket and pulled out his black, spiral-bound notepad. *Research telephone ring.* He flipped the pad closed, and returned it to his pocket. Maybe he could find the phone's manufacturer on the Web tonight at his rental. Case or no case, some things had to come first.

He'd learned his lesson. He'd get this little situation solved, criminals would be deposited in jail cleanly, and he'd do what he could to get back on James's good side. He knew she couldn't hold a grudge against him for too long. After all she'd mentored him since he left the Marines to join the Bureau.

He knew he'd really pissed the top lady off, parading those men through her office. But was it worth *this?*

As the newly hired security chief at P&L, he had an office to himself. He didn't know who to thank for that small favor. Outside stood rows and rows of battered metal desks without a single cubicle divider. How could the bankers get anything done? At some point, the walls had been painted a hue between blue and green. Why, he could only guess.

The whole place buzzed with nonstop corporate team building. If he heard one more inspiring little snippet over the office speaker, he'd cut the wires himself. As if the framed motivational posters weren't bad enough.

The FBI had lucked out when Arvest Lane had created the security position in the Gallem office. Over the course of the last six months, someone had been manipulating government money through P&L. Straight into a nice little offshore account.

Uncle Sam didn't like people to steal his money. Neither did Ward. Finding the culprit wouldn't be difficult. Just very, very time consuming with lots of paperwork. Yeah, James really knew how to turn the screws.

A week ago, Ward moved into the position, and no one in P&L knew his real identity. For all intents and purposes, he *was* the security chief, with all the perks, including access to the employee files. He'd read through them a dozen times. Searching for clues.

Hannah's rested on top. He lifted her résumé with the tiny photo of her stapled to the corner. The grainy picture was not the best quality. But it didn't obscure her high cheekbones or the lushness of her full lips. Lips that made a man's mind wonder.

Despite her beauty, her eyes were what always drew him. He wouldn't call them cold, but a coolness lingered in the green depths. When hounded by the male employees, she was quick with a glare of irritation. That was the only emotion she ever revealed.

Yet Hannah's eyes gave her away. Something… guarded some deep pain tinged those haunting eyes of hers. He planned to ferret out all her secrets.

First things first, assess the current situation. He wanted her. And even though they'd rarely made eye contact, he sensed she was attracted to him, and that it bothered her. A lot. A swell of satisfaction infused his gut. He liked the idea of her experiencing the same kind of frustration he did.

"Knock, knock." Ward glanced up to see his office visitor. He never really trusted a man who said *knock, knock* rather than actually knocking. Dan Protter, the Protter of Protter and Lane, walked through the door.

Ward schooled his features, cloaking himself in the persona of Ward Coleman. His new boss more than likely expected a man in charge of security to look, well, secure. Ward did his best to live up to the man's expectations.

In fact, strutting around the office acting macho, fulfilled his own dreams of what a federal agent should be doing. That lonely Marine lying in his bunk all those years ago had no idea that a fed's life wasn't so much chasing the bad guy and getting the girls. It was more about tackling a pile of paperwork and wrestling it to the ground. And there would be paperwork to spare with this P&L investigation.

But those times he did chase the bad guy made up for it all. The girl never stuck around for long. An odd twinge of disappointment surprised him. Whether the emotion came from the women not staying or the fact that he cared little if they did, he didn't know.

"TGIM, Ward." Dan handed Ward a coffee cup. "No cream, no sugar."

"Thanks." Ward never developed a liking for Mondays, or coffee, but he took a swig to satisfy Dan. He swallowed quickly. Coffee had about as much appeal to him as liquid dirt. Still, he did have a cover to keep, and this particular cover required him to act the tough guy. A guy who drank his coffee strong, preferably with the grounds still in.

Dan angled himself off Ward's desk. He sensed his new boss liked being around him. Ward's presence more than likely added a bit of danger in Dan's dully familiar world of investment banking. "I've gone over the new security measures you suggested," Dan said.

Though Ward's job was a means to an end, how could he leave here without implementing a few security procedures? He had standards, and leaving this particular job undone defied his sense of professionalism. Dan, and the rest of the investment firm, would luck out.

"The ID badges and password protection will work. But the new alarm system…we've got to keep our eye on the budget. Perhaps with a few well-written memos to the teams. Last year we left little notices in the break room. That solved the old food in the refrigerator problem quite nicely."

The various employees would be forever in Ward's debt if he prevented even one of P&L's infamous memos. He resisted the urge to ball his fists and forced a smile instead. "Dan, I've found the back door propped open twice now with a smashed soda can. The supply-room door is never shut and almost every employee in this office has a key to the outside fire door."

"We prefer team members. Remember, a sand castle is only as strong as every grain."

Good thing he'd already swallowed his coffee. He gestured outside his door with his cup. "There are over thirty team members out there who could care less about the half mil you've got socked away in equipment and supplies. An alarm and key card system is the only sure way of monitoring entry."

"Let's try the memo first."

Ward squared his shoulders ready to press his point. The leather from his shoulder holster poked him in the blade as he moved, reminding him why he was really here.

He settled back against the soft fabric of the executive chair. He sure didn't have anything like this kind of comfort in his office at the Bureau. Ward relaxed his shoulders. It wasn't as if this was his real job. No need to get worked up. If P&L wanted to open the window and strew cash bills into the wind, hey, it was their call.

Ah, but then this might actually settle out to his advantage. An idea popped into his head. "Why don't I meet with everyone on an individual basis? I'm new, and that would give me an opportunity to introduce myself, and share with each team member the importance of security."

"Good idea. We'll have a memo sent around right after lunch. Time to make some money." Dan picked up his coffee cup and left.

Ward shook his head. He'd read up on Dan Protter

before arriving. The man could make money the way other men made a mess in the sink. No effort and little worry. His problem was spending it. He had that fuzzy, can't-be-bothered-with-the-details genius about him.

It made him the perfect victim.

Good thing for Protter that Arvest Lane, based in Dallas, handled the administrative details of the partnership. The man was almost as bad as James in the paperwork department. There were tons of forms, often in triplicate. Ward guessed it was to make up for all the time without anyone in charge of security.

No wonder someone had taken to laundering money through Protter and Lane. The place was a security disaster waiting to happen. Since arriving in Gallem, he decided on two goals, find the pilferer and get to someplace cooler, like the equator.

Dan Protter had no clue, but Ward's initial investigation indicated an inside job. That was why he was here. And in most criminal cases, it all boiled down to the old saying…follow the money. Once he discovered the source of the money, that would lead him to the big crime. He just hoped James would let him have a crack at it once he completed this part of the investigation.

He wouldn't get that shot if he kept his mind on ice cubes. Or the sexy woman who ran them along her skin.

Ward returned his attention to the files on his desk with deliberation. Working frequently undercover, he was a man used to calculated focus.

He forced his eyes not to return to Hannah's picture, concentrating on the papers contained in the file instead. She worked as a computer programmer. He removed the paper clip, and flipped through the sheets of paper outlining her life.

Better than average grades. Member of the computer club. Several part-time jobs while in school. P&L was her third job out of college. Each job gave her added responsibility.

He leaned back in his chair and worked the paper clip between his fingers. Something bothered him. He couldn't place what. Something about Hannah's tidy résumé…

He twisted the pliable metal, then scanned the document again.

The job didn't suit her. Computers were all straight lines, numbers and cold machinery. None of that fit with Hannah. Her entire package exuded warm sensuality and curves. And melting ice cubes. The paper clip flicked off his thumb and glanced off the wall. He'd stretched the thing arrow straight. Not unlike him. Ward shifted in his seat to relieve some of the pressure the thought of dripping water added to his anatomy. His lower part.

If this were any normal assignment, he'd ask her out. Pursue her like any regular guy with a beating heart. But this wasn't any average assignment.

Not only was Hannah Garrett his object of sexual interest and infinite frustration, she was also his most likely suspect.

HANNAH FELT HIS EYES on her again. For a minute, she relished the awareness of him as a man. And her as a woman.

Since the new head of security had taken residence in the second corner office, she always seemed to be in his direct line of vision. The heavy sensation of being watched lasted long after she'd left his sight. Her shoulders tensed and her skin prickled just from getting a drink from the break room. One innocent moment of rubbing ice on her neck and...the warmth of a flush entered her cheeks. Just what she needed. More heat.

She hadn't even realized he could see her, but his door faced the little break room where employees stashed their drinks and warmed their food in the microwave. What kind of message did she send with that little display? The last thing she needed was to draw attention to herself. She'd be eating her lunch at her desk from now on.

Hannah sensed those sexy, cool green eyes of his missed nothing. Cool until they met hers. Then they misted into the color of the sea before a storm. Dangerous. Yet, she didn't always want to turn away from the tempest.

And that's where her new apprehension originated. She'd always been able to stamp out the barest hint of...of...she didn't even have a ready word to describe the feeling. Awareness?

No, no, no. Wariness was all she was experiencing.

Wariness was a familiar friend. She'd been on the alert for four years now. Sometimes, in the bright, revealing daylight of a lazy Saturday afternoon, she knew it would only be a matter of time before he caught up with her. The welcome of the enveloping night would ease her apprehension. Until the next sunrise.

She balled her fist, but resisted the urge to bang her hand on the table. Damn, she had thought she'd be safe in Gallem. The anonymity of the large metropolis promised her a level of freedom. Maybe a chance to have the semblance of a social life. She'd even toyed with the idea of dating or at least shooting for living the life of any normal, twenty-something girl in the city.

Hannah ached for that simple measure of security she hadn't had since she made the decision that changed her life.

Security. Her mind reeled back to Ward Coleman. With the ability to perform background checks, his job could be the perfect ruse for someone with an agenda. Someone looking to find her. Anxiety knotted the tiny muscles of her nape. She rolled her head side to side.

"Doing office yoga again?"

Hannah glanced up to see Dinah Wallace stroll in with her ever-present smile, waving a sheaf of paper. If Hannah were a different kind of person, Dinah would be gal-friend material. The kind to see chick flicks, talk about men and eat ice cream with when the romance turned sour. The kind of friend she yearned to have.

But she dared not get too close. One small slipup, and she'd be right back where she started. On the run. She couldn't afford it. Better to keep to herself. Better to ignore her longing for a good friend. Better to ignore any interest in a man. A man like Ward. A man offering the temptation of double danger.

Dinah plopped herself in the metal chair in front of Hannah's desk. Hannah had specifically chosen that chair so as not to invite lengthy visits to her office. Though the discomfort of the rigid metal seat never seemed to bother, Dinah, the office gossip.

"I don't know why you're in here eating tuna straight from the can, when you could be draping yourself in some sort of a seductive pose in the break room," Dinah said.

Since Ward's arrival, Dinah could think of little else other than devising ways to get the man's attention. Hannah had no intention of diverting the man's eyes to her. For her safety and sanity.

"I'm fine here," Hannah told her.

Dinah knocked on the desk. "Hello. You're not getting the point. There's a man across from the break room."

Hannah tried for a casual shrug. "There are lots of guys in the office."

"You made the point yourself. Guy versus man. This one's all man. I can almost see the muscles rippling under his suit jacket. Muscles he earned doing strapping manly things. He's no banker in love with his latest investment."

"Not interested." Hannah picked up her fork, scooped out another bite of tuna and shoved it into her mouth. That should prove her tuna over man point quite nicely.

"What a waste. Especially since you're the only one in the office Mr. Security seems to have any interest in."

The fork slipped through her fingers and banged against her desk with a tattling clang. A tickle of excitement fluttered in her chest.

Dinah laughed and graced her with a smug smile. "Yeah, you just blew your cover. Admit it, you're not so immune to Mr. Green Eyes with the tight—"

"No, I'm just surprised is all."

She'd suspected the new security head had been paying a little closer attention to her. Up until now, she mentally filed it under her natural inclination toward suspicion. And to be honest, she tried to convince herself maybe his long stares might indicate a little sexual interest, as well. A tiny thrill of anticipation coursed through her until she tamped it down in a hurry. What sort of luck was this? To finally be attracted to a man who could possibly be here to harm her. His arrival seemed too sudden. His interest in her too immediate.

Dinah's announcement confirmed her acquired inclination to be on alert. She had to play down her clumsy reaction. She forced a tight smile. Maybe it would be to her advantage to let her friend think she found the man attractive. Not much of a stretch. Maybe it would keep Dinah's suspicions centered on a target Hannah could control better. "Well, I—"

"I knew it. I knew you liked him."

Hannah settled against the cushion of her chair, and let her friend take it from there.

Dinah crossed her legs and began swaying them in excitement. "I don't know why I didn't see it before. You're shy. I mean it all fits. You're the computer gal. You do most of your work from home or on weekends. I'm surprised you're even here today. You're not comfortable around men."

Oh, if only Dinah knew the whole of that story.

Hannah shifted in her chair. "Even if I were interested in the man, which I'm not, parading myself in the break room is out of the question. It has something to do with decorum."

"Remind me to look that word up in the dictionary later."

Hannah wadded up her napkin and threw it at her friend. "You're impossible. And I'm not uncomfortable around men. Protter and Lane have a very clear policy on intraoffice dating. I've received several memos to the effect."

"Oh, puhleez. I think you're the only person that doesn't immediately put those gems in the circular file. And office policy still doesn't explain your general lack of presence around this place. Not that I can blame you. Take a peek at your office. Where are the pictures? Where's the dead plant? You don't have a single doodad on your desk. You're also the only person who's left all those silly inspirational sayings on the wall."

"I kind of like them."

Dinah gave her a look somewhere between disbelief and disgust. She pointed to the poster to her left. "It Only Takes One Ember To Make A Blaze? Whatever."

Dinah rolled her eyes, and Hannah couldn't help but laugh.

"When is Protter going to figure out what we really need is a raise? Or maybe just a casual day other than when it's a thousand degrees outside. I think not wearing hose, and having to visit the dry cleaners every other week is worth the piddly cost-of-living increase he gave us last year."

Hannah hadn't been at P&L last year. With the tantalizingly dangerous new presence of the head of security, she might not be much longer this year, either. First she needed to redirect Dinah's thoughts.

She tugged the pager off her waistband, and tossed it on the table. "I don't have to be in the office to do my job. I'm always available. The server pages me when it goes down. Besides, it's easier for me to do my work at nights and on weekends for one simple reason. You all aren't here to mess everything up. You take one measly computer class, and you think you can fiddle with the parameters. Settings changed. Passwords lost."

"You're never going to let me live down the password thing, are you?"

"It was three passwords. Three in one day."

Dinah waved the paper at her. "You're getting me completely off course on the whole reason for my visit. Latest memo from human resources."

Hannah took the paper from her and scanned it.

"I'll leave you to devour the contents later. I'll just give you the highlights. Boss man has a new decree. Better get over the shy thing with Ward Coleman."

"Why?"

"Because later you get to meet with him face-to-face."

2

WARD KNEW WHEN he was being avoided.

A woman avoided a man for only two reasons. She either didn't want him, or she wanted him bad. Okay, not rocket science, but it had worked since he'd hit nineteen, and managed to figure out a few things about women, other than the obvious.

And the obvious was Hannah wanted him B-A-D. She'd also stretched avoidance to Olympic proportions. It didn't take a federal agent to spot the ducking-into-a-doorway routine.

Two could play. In fact, one of Ward's favorite pastimes was toying with the bad guy. Or in this case, girl. In the last two days, he'd made a special point of getting in her way. When Hannah poured her morning coffee in the break room, he held the sugar. When she made a few copies, he, being the new guy around, always needed help with the machine. And oh, his password. How many times had he forgotten it? And when he asked for her to write it down, he got a sample of her handwriting as well as her fingerprints.

This case should be a piece of cake. One more week

to ferret out the culprit, another week or so of tracing all the wire transfers, searching through the files and generally doing all the paperwork he hated. He'd discovered something about investment bankers; they liked a lot of paper. A lovefest of forms. Which meant he'd have to spend a lot of time doing the tedious cataloging of evidence.

Ward studied his appointment list. Most of the employees had eagerly met with him to discuss security issues. Except Hannah. But she couldn't avoid him today, even though she'd signed up for the last possible time slot on the last possible day.

Ward glanced at the clock, which indicated he had to wait only another five minutes before his reckoning with Hannah.

Anticipation made his muscles tighten. Not much longer and he'd have Hannah all to himself. He'd be able to question her without evasion, hear the sexy huskiness of her voice. Meet the green of her eyes.

He'd already narrowed his search to three individuals with access to the computer system. As head of those computer systems, Hannah had designed the very software someone was using to launder the money.

Would Hannah blatantly use her own software? Wouldn't make much sense. She struck him as one smart lady. But then the security was so lax at P&L, it was only a matter of time before someone took advantage of it. Was that someone Hannah Garrett?

Something in his gut told him…damn. That was the problem. When it came to her, he had nothing. Zilch. Oh, he had a lot of gut reactions where Hannah was concerned, but not a single clue as to what made the lady tick. Frustrated, he curled his fingers around the edges of her résumé. He'd looked at the thing half a dozen times. He quelled the urge to crush it into a ball.

Okay, maybe things weren't all bad. He did have a gut reaction with her work history. It was perfect. College placement counselors could teach a course with it. And there lay the problem. He scanned the text again. He knew the answer to Hannah's secrets hid in what the brief bio didn't tell.

A soft knock drew his attention away from the paper and to the very person occupying his thoughts. For a moment, he didn't breathe. Framed in the door, Hannah didn't appear so mysterious. He still wanted her. She'd mastered her red curls into that neat knot she liked. He still wanted her. Her strong features remained expressionless, and she'd plopped a pair of dark-framed glasses on her nose. He still wanted her. She radiated the very picture of a professional computer programmer...and he still wanted her.

She radiated the very picture of a very irritated professional computer programmer. She tapped her pencil against the notepad in a cadence that suggested she wouldn't mind flinging the pencil at his face. Hard.

He smiled at her.

The pencil tapped harder.

She took several graceful steps into the room, and sat in the chair he indicated. Efficient and professional. Once again her green eyes gave her away. With a touch of surprise, he noted they weren't the clear green he'd expected. A cloudiness masked the rich verdant hue. All the better to conceal.

Ward widened his smile to a nice open invitation. "I'm glad you joined me."

"I didn't have much choice."

He smiled again. She resumed the tapping. "It won't be that bad, most people have given me excellent suggestions for improving security."

"This meeting isn't necessary. I already outlined all my suggestions in a memo to Mr. Protter. I CC'd human resources and you."

Ah, yes. The neatly typed pages he'd placed with his handwritten notes. He had to appear as if he were doing true work while here undercover. Actually, her suggestions were quite good, but then, a criminal would know the best ways to rip off a place.

He nodded. "I prefer to meet one-on-one. Brainstorming will often raise possibilities neither one of us would have thought of on our own. Almost a get-to-know-you-better kind of session. Why don't you tell me a little more about yourself?"

She gave him a wary glance, alerting his hunter-agent instincts. He recognized that look. It was the kind that proved she'd faced inquisitors before and knew she didn't have to say or do a thing. At least not without a lawyer present.

He closed the file. He had his answer. Hannah Garrett not only remained a legitimate suspect, but now she moved to the front of the pack. He felt a surge of disappointed satisfaction. Until this moment, he hadn't even realized he'd held some pathetic hope he'd sized up the situation completely wrong, and she was just some gal who liked computers and needed a date for Saturday night.

The lights flickered, and the pitiful excuse for an air conditioner Protter had installed whined to a halt. "That's just great. I didn't think this place could get much hotter."

Hannah pulled out a frilly white cloth and blotted her forehead. She had the flushed, gently perspired look a woman wears after being made love to. That she even possessed the lacy handkerchief not only surprised him, but also it was sexy as hell. Hot desire slammed his body. He searched for some indication that Hannah was suffering as he was. That, at least, would make his perpetual hard-on somewhat worth it.

Why did she wear so many clothes? And such ugly ones. The brown sack of a skirt left nothing for his active imagination to latch on to. Couldn't she wear something a little more formfitting? Or something anyway that didn't end at the knee.

"Didn't you get the shorts memo from human resources?" he asked. "You must be on fire in all those clothes."

Hannah straightened, then replaced the handkerchief in her pocket and crossed her legs. The pencil resumed its tapping accompanied by the obviously irritated swinging of her leg. He didn't care. Each swing gave him a peekaboo view of something other than the smooth skin of her ankle. Her ankles, as ankles went, were outstanding. Only he wanted to see more.

"I really don't think my clothes should be of any concern to the head of security."

"Suit yourself." Ward fluffed his cotton T-shirt in a vain attempt to get a little more air onto his overheated skin. Hannah averted her eyes quickly. He hid a grin. Ahh, maybe it was more than just the heat affecting Hannah. He flexed his muscles a bit as he reached for his notepad.

"Now then, tell me the procedure for ensuring out-siders are not accessing the computer system."

Hannah stopped the tapping and leaned forward. Her green eyes darkened. The first bit of passion he'd seen. "That falls under my job description. I don't see where that's any of your business."

"All areas of security are my business."

Her eyes narrowed, but the passion he'd spotted earlier faded. Damn. What had been there? She looked down, angled herself away from him and blocked her body with the notepad. All signs of criminal intent. Or that she just didn't like him. Nah.

He'd thrown her off balance.

Now, he needed to figure out why. And do it again. Was it because he challenged her job performance? Or because he questioned how outsiders were able to access computers? Time to rattle her some more.

"Tell me how—"

The lights flickered again. A grinding, mechanical screech wrenched through the office. Then complete darkness.

For a moment the entire floor housing Protter and Lane lay silent. Then a few chuckles and squeals drifted in from the outer office. Hannah released a soft sigh, and the tension strung between them slackened.

"You okay?" he asked.

"Sure."

Her voice vibrated with a loose quality he hadn't heard from her since they'd first met. Weird. Instead of making her more nervous, the darkness almost seemed to make Hannah more relaxed. At least the tapping pencil had stopped.

Peeps and chirps sounded outside his window. The power failure had not affected the bird family who'd nested on his ledge. At least his sliver of a window provided a little light.

He stood and felt his way around the corners of his desk. A shrill siren sounded and the emergency security light beamed red in her face.

Ward reached for her. She wrenched away from his touch. "Hey, I'm just taking you to the window."

With an abrupt, almost violent lurch, she stood. "No. Don't touch me."

He raised his hands and stepped away. Her notepad slid to the floor, and they both hunkered down to retrieve it.

Her fingers wrapped around the steel spiral of the notebook just as his hand met hers. The soft smooth skin beneath his fingers warmed him. Her shoulders shook as she sucked in a breath.

Then, with a determination that radiated from her to him, he felt her fortify her strength. The unease he'd sensed when the light had glared into her face vanished. She was completely under control.

The siren stopped as the lights flickered back on. They remained crouched by his desk. She, holding the notepad. He, holding her hand.

He gazed into her eyes. Although her back stretched strong and firm, her green eyes still held the uneasiness she'd shown moments ago. "I'm sorry. I didn't mean to startle you."

Her green eyes flashed, a hint of gold burned like a bursting ember. He sensed something in the fiery depths. An unflinching vulnerability. Those two descriptions countered each other so completely that he stiffened like a man who realized he'd stopped making sense. A condition usually brought on by a woman.

The flash in her eyes disappeared, but the damage was done. Her brief yield had stirred up a primeval response. Shocked by the heat of his reaction, his hand dropped from the satiny skin of her hand.

Hannah stood and smoothed her skirt into place. Total concealment. He sat back on his heels and watched her race away.

Now more than ever he needed to know her secrets.

He could afford to bide his time. In two days it would be Saturday. He'd have her in the office all to himself.

HANNAH PADDED barefoot into her kitchen and spooned coffee into the basket. Her mind drifted to work as she waited for the coffee to brew.

She smelled a setup. Since her disastrous meeting with the security head on Thursday, it seemed she couldn't evade him. The last thing she wanted was to be anywhere near the watchful gaze of Ward Coleman. Wherever she went…there he was. All six foot plus of outstanding male.

A delicious shiver went down her back. It had been

so long. So long since she'd felt the steady warmth of a man's hand. So long since she'd felt the mind-numbing pleasure of a man's touch. So long since she'd hungered for a man. And she hungered for Ward Coleman.

And he wasn't doing much to help her out. She couldn't get a pencil out of the supply closet without him retrieving a pen. Forget about the break room. She hadn't been there since the beginning of the week. And Friday was doughnut day, and the boss had sprung for Krispy Kreme. Coleman was gonna pay for that one.

The only place she could find any peace was in the ladies' room, and Friday afternoon she could have sworn she saw him skulking by the men's room across the hall.

But today was Saturday. Her special time alone in the office. No one asking for their password, no one complaining about the server being too slow. *No one.* In an hour, it would be just her, blank disks and a computer to back up.

She leaned against the counter and took in her tiny kitchen. She loved it. It was the first one she'd had with a dishwasher. Why she'd stupidly avoided having one until this point she didn't know. Her foster mother's hands had always been rough and red from soapy water. A woman's hands were meant for something other than cleaning. Her mind always knew it, but she'd only recently put it into practice when she spotted the box of dishwasher detergent the landlord's wife had left.

She tugged the lapels of her green terry cloth robe tighter. The blistering heat wave passing through

Gallem hadn't reached full strength yet, so she could relax fully covered. Saturday morning always seemed to start out right with a cup of coffee and the newspaper in her kitchen.

The apartment had practically rented itself after she saw it. The previous tenants had been a couple of college kids. They'd sponge painted the walls black, and the elderly landlord had knocked off twenty bucks a month so he wouldn't have to repaint. She kind of liked it. The front room reminded her of a dark, moonless night. She'd placed a few stick-on stars on the ceiling for effect.

Furniture remained a luxury. She didn't have much left, leaving almost everything she'd accumulated behind in the last town she'd been relocated to. It was bad to get attached to stuff anyway. She'd found a few good pieces for this new place—a sturdy couch; she'd fashioned a slipcover for it with a navy flat sheet covered with yellow moons and suns. It kept with the space theme. Maybe she should have stuck with plain navy, but then a voice in her head said it was time to delve into the light.

She hadn't yet found a reasonable kitchen table, but she had unearthed two bar stools, badly needing attention. She'd spent an entire weekend sanding and staining, then proudly placed them before the nice, neutral Formica dining bar.

Hannah slid onto the bar stool and tucked her legs beneath her. She reached for her coffee, inhaled the warm, toasty aroma and took a sip. *Ahhh.* With lazy fingers she folded the newspaper flat on the countertop.

The date lurched. Bold and warning.

Her breath left her body with a whoosh.

June twenty-first. The longest day of the year. How could she have forgotten?

She gulped down some more coffee, coughing as it slid down into her lungs instead of her throat.

How she hated this date. When light seemed to take over the night. The calendar explained it all. The impending sense of doom, the anxiety, her paranoia of Ward.

It wasn't Ward Coleman and the exciting yet dangerous promise she'd glimpsed in his eyes at all. It was the date that had her jangly with nerves.

The longest day of the year had been the last day of her normal life.

Hannah drew in a calming breath the way the counselors had taught her to four years ago. She would beat this. She was beating this. Nothing special lay in the date. It was no different from the twentieth. Or the first. Or the thirteenth.

No. The date held no meaning for her. Not anymore.

She slammed the paper to the table and marched into her bedroom. She nearly tripped on the inflatable mattress. Not that it would have been too great a loss if she'd popped it. But she would be kind of sad. The convenient mattress was one of her few possessions to last through two moves.

The accordion door of her closet slapped against the wall. She'd yanked it harder than she'd intended. With a jerk, she grabbed a long skirt and blouse. No way would she crumble under the weight of the date.

Hannah Garrett was made of stronger stuff, and she would go to the office as usual. Maybe the next time Ward Coleman got in her way, she'd smile at him.

"YOU GOTTA SEE THIS, WARD. Some reporter is actually out there trying to see if the sidewalk is hot enough to fry an egg."

Ward looked up from his review of the three suspect files and at his best friend, Brett Haynes, gaping out the fourteenth-story window. "Don't they have any real news?"

"This is the only news," Brett pointed out. "Sixty-eight days of no rain coupled with this unbearable heat—it's a disaster waiting to happen. A local news channel's dream."

"Speaking of unbearable, isn't it about time for you to call home again?" Ward asked.

Brett glanced at his watch. "No, I'm not supposed to call until—" His friend wore the expression that indicated he just realized he was the butt of a joke. "Hey, we're not that bad."

Ward laughed. "No, what was bad was when she put the baby on the phone."

"Just wait. Your time will come."

"Ahh, but you forget. I'm the man women love to leave. Besides, I can't think of a worse thing than being trapped behind a desk at the Bureau with you."

"They leave because you make them want to leave. By the way, the guys asked me to give you these." Brett dumped a package of condoms on Ward's desk.

With the tip of his pen, Ward flicked them at his

friend. "What are you crazy? Put those away, some-one's going to see you."

"There's no one here. Put 'em in your wallet. It's time you joined the land of the living." Brett puffed up his shirt. "At least I'm not stuck in this oven. Why didn't you tell me the place was so hot?"

"I did mention James had relegated me to hell. Besides they're about to close the whole place down—" he glanced down at his watch "—in about another hour." Where *was* Hannah?

"Is that why the area is deserted? As I drove in, I felt like I'd stepped into one of those sci-fi movies where all the inhabitants of a city had disappeared."

Ward nodded. "Since it's the weekend and so hot, the city officials are going to divert as much of the electric-ity as they can out of the city and to the suburbs."

"And since only an idiot would waste a Saturday in the office, the powers-that-be thought 'who'd care?'"

"They think that might prevent an overall power outage," Ward said.

"How?"

"Something about power grids and diversions. I don't know, I'm an agent, not an engineer."

"I think that line works better when you're a doctor. If the place is going to shut down, what are we still doing here? This weekend was all about beer and baseball."

The outer office door opened and closed.

Hannah.

Ward stood and went around the desk to his door. "Right on time."

"On time for what?"

"My number-one suspect. Hannah?" he called out in his most surprised voice.

Hannah turned and faced him, not bothering to hide her disappointment. With a quick glance, he sized her up. Even though she knew no one would be in the office, she still wore that long skirt.

But glorious red hair lay in waves down her back. He stifled a groan. He'd have an image of Hannah's hair strewn on his pillow burned in his brain for the rest of the day. Week. Forever.

Wait a minute, something was missing. Something in her eyes. She didn't leave him much time to ponder the absence because she strolled right toward him. Another thing she'd never done.

"What are you doing here?" she asked.

Okay, some of the same old suspicious Hannah remained. This was a reaction he could appreciate. A prickle of relief eased his shoulders. He hadn't even realized he tensed them.

"Oh, I have an old buddy visiting me. Hannah, this is Brett."

She cut Brett a glance. "Nice to meet you. Too bad you got here just in time for all the heat."

"And it just keeps getting hotter," Brett added.

Ward shot him a warning glance, then cleared his throat. "I was showing Brett my new office."

Hannah returned her attention to Ward and smiled at him. And Ward dropped his pen.

"Bye, guys. Off to back up the hard drives." She gave them a little finger wave, and they watched as she walked into her office and closed the door.

After retrieving his pen from the floor, he saw Brett was shaking his head. "What?"

"You're going to have a heck of a time proving this one innocent."

"What are you talking about? I'm here to find the bad guy and put him *or her* in jail."

"Yeah. Sure. Just keep telling yourself that. It may actually help for a while. But I recognize the signs. It's benched many a great agent."

THAT FELT GOOD. Hannah had never turned the tables on someone before, and seeing Ward Coleman drop his pen at her feet…it was almost worth the intrusion on her Saturday.

She opened her desk drawer, pulled the rewritable CD from its sleeve and stuck it into the computer. With a few clicks of her mouse, the backup process began. With the expected lulls in power, this particular backup was crucial. She snapped open the top of her diet cola, retrieved the book from her purse and began to read.

Hard work indeed.

Her thoughts kept drifting back to Ward. She closed the book on her thumb and stared at the cover picture. The hero of the book was a pirate. He possessed Ward's green eyes and blond hair, and strong jaw. Was that why she'd bought the romantic pirate story? Did she see Ward in the brave man pictured on the cover?

Of course not. She simply found herself sexually attracted to him. It was natural. She *was* a grown woman who'd denied herself for a long time. An unsteady desire settled in her as she remembered Ward looking into her eyes. For a brief moment, she'd been tempted. The pull of his attraction had her melting faster than an ice cream in the Gallem sun.

Ward no. Pirate yes. And she opened her book.

The pager at her waist vibrated as the pirate in her book hoisted the heroine into his arms. Her fingers shook as she replaced the bookmark and set the book on her desk.

No one except her boss at P&L or the server had her pager number. No one except her contacts.

She ripped the black standard-issue pager from her skirt. She didn't recognize the number, but an asterisk blinked as the last character on the miniscreen.

The symbol for danger.

Using the private phone in her office could prove too risky. Anyone at the switchboard would be able to see the flashing light of her line and know it was in use. Then there was the possibility of someone listening in....

With trembling legs, she grabbed her purse and walked toward the fire stairwell. Once the door slammed behind her, she sprinted down three flights. From her previous scouting, she knew no one milled about on a Saturday on this floor housing law offices. The attorneys had installed a pay phone near the public restroom to prevent clients from asking to make personal calls.

Hannah found her change, inserted it into the phone and punched in the number. She'd gone through this drill before, but her nerves never got any better.

The person on the other end answered the line on the first ring. "Code?"

"726418," she recited. Hannah knew that code number the way others knew the digits of their social security number.

"Kyle Barton escaped from prison this morning."

Gasping, Hannah nearly dropped the receiver. Her stomach quaked, and she gulped several breaths to keep from losing her breakfast.

The date. The longest day of the year. The day that started it all. Of course this would be the day Kyle made a break for freedom. He'd see the irony and run with it. Why had she mocked it earlier? Dared the calendar to mean anything. He'd always find her. Kyle had promised that after the police had placed the cuffs on his hands and escorted him from the courtroom. He'd find her just as surely as day following night. It was her destiny. As it was his.

Okay, stop it. There was no such thing as destiny. That was the kind of stuff Kyle had said to an impressionable girl just wanting to please. *Be practical.*

A dozen questions came to mind. How had he escaped? Why hadn't he been restrained? She sucked in a breath, and shrank into the shadows.

"There's no reason to suspect you're compromised. What are you doing now?"

"Backing up the computers. I do it every Saturday. I'm almost done."

"Good. Keep with your routine. Finish up and go home. Don't draw any attention to yourself. You know the routine."

Yeah, she knew the routine.

"Marshals are tracking him right now, but we want you to lie low. Do you have some sick days coming?"

"Yes," she answered, her voice as scratchy as sandpaper. But she knew. He'd find her. He always did.

"Good. Take the days and get out of sight. Fly below the radar. If I call again, it's to give you the address of a safe house. If he's captured, you'll see it on TV." Her contact hung up.

Hannah replaced the receiver, and checked for the weapon in her purse. She carried a Taser. Even though she would have preferred her gun, no one thought anything of a single woman with a Taser in her purse.

The man who had vowed to see her dead was free.

Hurry the night. Safety lay in the shadows.

3

"Ms. Garrett, what are you still doing here?"

Hannah looked up from the computer with a start. It was Frank, the elderly security guard for the sixteen-story building. Not a threat.

Don't draw any attention to yourself.

She offered what she hoped wasn't too tentative a smile. "Hi, Frank. Must have lost track of the time. I wanted to back up these hard drives before the power outage."

"Well, you gotta get out of here. They're about to blow the horns."

Darn, she'd forgotten they'd be doing that. This power diversion couldn't come at a worse time. She glanced at the progress bar. Still at least three minutes until the backup was complete. "I'm about to shut off the computer."

"Do it quickly. Glad I decided to do one more walk through the building. Found your new security guy here and a doctor down on three."

"Thanks, Frank. I'll get out of here now."

The security guard looked relieved. He must have expected an argument. "Good. They're gonna blast the tornado sirens as a final warning. If you hear those, you better clear out."

Those sirens, a necessity in tornado alley where Gallem was located, were only used in extreme cases other than their original use. This electrical shutdown was serious business. She looked at her watch. She was cutting it closer than she liked, but she still had plenty of time to get to her car and drive out of the parking garage.

Finally, the backup was done, and she quickly clicked Shut Down. Hannah waved as Frank hurried off, then grabbed her purse, stuffed in her paperback and snapped it shut. She'd love a quick trip to the ladies' room to pat a bit of cool water onto her cheeks and behind her neck. She couldn't remember a time when she'd felt so hot.

But she wouldn't risk it. After walking to the lobby, she pressed the elevator button with a relieved jab. Leaving the downtown area this late was a big mistake, but Saturdays were the only time she could back up the server without Protter and Lane losing a lot of money. And with a definite power outage, that backup was a necessity.

The sirens began their slow buildup to a loud warning. She was quite used to alarms warning of tornadoes. The sound never failed to fill her with dread and spurred her to speed up. She checked her watch and eyed the stairwell. According to her watch, she still had five minutes. Hiking down fourteen flights of stairs held little appeal.

The ding of the elevator signaled its arrival, ending

her decision. She entered with a grateful quick step. She fluffed her shirt to cool a bit. The building maintenance obviously had the air-conditioning on efficiency mode.

Ice cream. Cold, melting ice cream would help cool her off. Too bad she wouldn't be able to eat it on her balcony as the sun set. Her favorite time of the day.

The temperature would probably still hover around the ninety-degree mark. But it did remind her to stop by the grocery store. She'd need to stock up. No telling how long she'd have to stay holed up in her apartment.

The doors had almost closed when a large, masculine hand pried them apart. Hannah moved until her back pressed against the cool, faux wood.

"I see I'm not alone in waiting until the last minute," Ward said.

Her hand automatically went to her purse, and she wrapped her fingers around the comforting presence of her Taser. One thing she'd learned in these last four years on the run, life did have its ironies. Thirty minutes ago, she'd entertained pirate thoughts about the man. Now she wondered if he were sent here to find her and bring her to Kyle. That burly-looking friend of Ward's, Brett, had that capable rough appearance about him. As did Ward.

He turned away. She switched the Taser safety off with her thumb. Just a few more seconds and the doors would slide open, and she could head for her car.

With a slow swoosh the elevator came to a stop. The jerk of the emergency brakes engaging knocked her slightly off balance. She dropped her purse to the floor. A small red emergency light fluttered in the corner for a moment, then puttered out.

Utter darkness draped them.

The electricity had shut off early.

She chased her purse to the floor. Panicked, she felt the floor for the spilled contents. The Taser was her only weapon. She heard it rolling on the floor. "Why'd that red light go out?" she asked.

"Damn building maintenance."

A high-pitched ringing filled her ears. Had Ward and his friend rigged the elevator? Now would be his chance. His chance to bring her to Kyle. Or bring her body.

Beside her, Ward cursed. "This is all I need."

She sucked in a deep breath and tried to take a cue from Ward. He only sounded irritated. She counted to ten.

Then to twenty.

Though he didn't act or sound like a man who was ready to kill her, she didn't plan on sticking around to find out. She silently recited the mantra she'd been given. *When confronted, act.*

Swallowing her anxiety, she quelled the shaking of her hands as she felt her way along the wall to where she hoped the emergency phone was.

Bingo! Her fingers brushed over the bumpy Braille on the buttons. She moved lower. The cool, smooth metal beneath her fingertips indicated she'd found the control panel. Usually, the emergency phone lay below.

Her nails clicked on the metal handle. She yanked it open. The cordless receiver fell to the floor with a clunk. "Oh no."

"Don't tell me that was the phone."

Taking a deep calming breath, she patted the floor for

the useless device. His voice didn't sound threatening.
*Take it easy. Maybe he's just a normal guy. A guy with
bad luck...just like you.* "Yes. Maintenance strikes again."

She heard him fumble in the darkness. "I have my
cell phone. Hope the battery is charged."

He laughed. She prayed that was his idea of a joke
and not a real worry. But she did breath a little easier.
If he and his buddy had rigged the elevator, he'd be
subduing her right now, not trying to find a way to get
out. Right?

A rush of relief filled her as she heard the beeps on his
phone. She could handle being inside their steel cage as
long as she knew it would be for just a few minutes more.

"Damn it."

Her heart began to pound. "What's wrong?"

"I'm getting nothing but static. Can't get a signal in
the middle of all these steel office towers. Being inside
an elevator doesn't help."

A nauseating sense of apprehension invaded her, but
she wouldn't sit there like a helpless victim. She had to
do something.

Hannah stood and felt her way to the elevator doors.
She balled up her fists and began to pound. "Hey,
someone. We're trapped. Help!"

Her fellow captive joined her. How long they stood
together pummeling the door, she didn't know. Soon
the force behind his blows weakened, and her voice
grew hoarse.

Her legs wobbled, and she sank to the floor, sliding
along the smoothness of the elevator wall. "This is useless."

"Yeah," he said. "Everyone is long gone." The silence stretched between them for a moment. "Hey, look on the bright side."

"What?"

"The phone's buttons provide a little bit of light."

She licked her dry lips. "You're taking this too calmly. Who knows how long we'll be here tonight."

"Brett's expecting me, and he knows where I was last. When I don't answer my phone, he'll come to find out why."

Maybe Ward was just the head of security. Maybe Brett was just a buddy. Maybe.

"What about you? Anyone waiting for you at home?" he asked.

That was a loaded question. Was he trying to size up the enemy or was he simply forming a plan?

The memory of his long, hot stares assaulted her. Maybe he was asking out of a personal interest. Her heart beat faster at the thought. Dare she tell him the truth?

She closed her eyes and shook her head. No one.

"Hannah?"

"What?"

"Is anyone expecting you?"

Did she trust Ward? Could she trust him? "Uh, no, sorry."

Silence stretched between them. Had she miscalculated? Was he preparing to swoop down on her? The smooth glide of fabric sliding against the wall filled the compartment. The wall opposite her. Ward must have decided to sit on the floor, too. "I don't want to think what kind of germs are on this floor."

Sweet relief poured through her, causing a cooling sweat to break out on the back of her neck.

She rubbed her eyes wishing for something to appear. "I can't see a thing. Why won't my eyes adjust?"

"Your eye requires light. The light rays send electrical signals to the brain where the image is then decoded."

"Translation please?"

"Your eyes won't adjust, it's too dark."

"Great. How'd you know that?"

"Spent many a night in the jungle as a Marine."

"Really?"

"Hoo-Raa."

Hannah allowed herself to smile. He wouldn't be able to see her anyway. Ward was what he appeared to be. A former Marine and the head guy of security. Her pirate image flashed again. Yeah, Marines did a lot for water.

"Don't worry, once it gets dark, Brett will know something's wrong," he said.

She exhaled a slow breath. "Today's the summer solstice. The longest day of the year."

"So I guess our wait will be even longer."

"It's kind of ironic. From our more pagan past, the solstice was a celebration of light."

Ward laughed. "And we're stuck in the dark."

Disappointment layered on top of her apprehension. "Some people believe it's a time for renewal."

"There's a joke there somewhere." The man beside her sighed. "We might be here for a while. What can we do for fun?"

One thing about pirates. They sometimes had wicked ideas. Or in this case, inspired them.

"You'll feel better if you take off a few clothes," Ward said a while later. He'd already shucked his shirt, shoes and socks.

Perspiration rolled down her temple. She gave a nervous laugh. "I think I'll hold out as long as I can."

The elevator had become a steamy box and she felt like a wilting, hothouse weed. She pulled the wispy material of her skirt over her calves. She couldn't read her watch, but guessed there were still several hours of daylight left. No telling how much longer they'd have to sit here.

He shifted across from her, but her heart didn't race in alarm. Although it did race. Over the last four years, she'd learned to ratchet up her instinct, recoiling from even the most casual contact or closeness. Yet with Ward, her usual skittishness diminished.

"I can't take it anymore. I'm getting out of these shorts." Ward stood, sending a whoosh of air floating her way. She heard the clink of metal against metal as he unlooped his belt. She clenched her eyes tight as she waited for the next sound—the zip of his fly coming down. A ringing began in her ears. His shorts hit the floor with a thud, and she sensed him stepping out of them. He tossed his clothes to the side.

"Ah," he said.

She nearly groaned, and tried not to imagine what he'd look like. Tall, muscular, and wearing only his Skivvies. If Marines wore such a thing. His presence had dwarfed her as they'd stood together, pounding uselessly against the elevator door. His presence beside her felt…masculine. Despite the heat, her nipples tightened.

She fluffed her shirt again. The darkness concealed many things. Thankfully.

"I bet you're rubbing that dimple in your chin." Ward's voice carried over to her, melting like butter.

"It's called a cleft and I've always hated it."

"Why?"

"It's boyish."

Ward laughed. It was a warm chuckle deep from his chest. Great, there were those shaky knees again. How could he do that to her with just a laugh? "There's nothing boyish about you, Hannah."

A sensuous curl of awareness tickled her senses. She tread on dangerous territory here. Ward was way out of her league. Actually, she didn't even belong in a league. She should never have attempted that smile. Time for some evasive maneuvers. "I'm getting a little hungry. Do you have any food in your briefcase?"

A long pause followed her question. She held her breath.

"I'll check."

She released her breath on a quiet sigh and reached for her purse. Perhaps she still had some airline peanuts from a trip a few weeks ago. She thought longingly of the candy bar she had stashed in her desk drawer.

"Found it." The click of his briefcase opening filled the tiny compartment. "We're in luck. I thought I might have a water bottle in here. Last night I left my gym bag in the locker and stashed my water in here. Not much left, we'll have to ration."

"It's okay, I'm not overly thirsty right now. Somehow knowing we have it makes it better." She twisted and her blouse stuck to her back. If she didn't cool down, she'd be in a whole lot of trouble. Ward seemed to be faring better, but then he'd taken off most of his clothes. If not all.

Enticing images came to mind. Ward had that wavy kind of hair that made him not mind if a woman wanted to run her fingers through it. Kyle had hated her touching his hair, messing it up. He liked to keep it under control.

As much as she would like to deny it, something about Ward drew her, common sense shouted "Run Away!" But every one of her nerve endings shouted back they wanted to be touched. And to touch.

The man oozed raw sexual energy.

Another bead of perspiration rolled down the side of her face. She had to do it. She had to strip.

If she took off one item of clothing slowly, perhaps it would seem more of a treat that way. She'd start with her slip. What a stupid piece of clothing that was anyway.

She stood, and hiked up her skirt. Heat filled her cheeks even though she knew Ward couldn't see her actions. There was something very intimate about stripping before a man. A tremor of excitement raced through her as she eased the silky material down her hips.

"Finally got hot enough, huh?"

She stopped abruptly, the material at her knees. Despite the utter darkness, she felt his eyes on her. On her body. Even with the stifling heat, her nipples hardened.

Stop it, you're being ridiculous. She kicked off her shoes and stepped out of the hot fabric, tossing it into the corner. "Something like that."

The air brushed against her thighs, giving her a moment of blessed relief. And a burst of energy. "Don't most elevators have escape hatches? I've seen them in movies."

Ward stood beside her. "I didn't get a good visual before the lights went out. I've probably been in this elevator half a dozen times and I have no idea. But it's worth a shot. I'll loop my hands together and give you a boost up."

"What?"

"I'm not tall enough to reach. Grab my hand."

All the comfortable feelings she'd garnered to this point vanished. She'd have to touch him. Feel the heat of his bare skin. The tightness of his muscles beneath her fingertips.

She thrust out her hand in the general direction of Ward's voice.

His long fingers clasped hers and drew her toward him. He placed her hand on his shoulder and stooped. "Use your hand for leverage and lift your foot."

His skin felt smooth and, oh so inviting, as she curled her hand around his shoulder. The muscles beneath her fingertips tensed slightly as she braced herself against him. His breath ruffled the material of her blouse.

"That's it, now lift your foot."

She lifted her leg and bumped her calf into his hands. He slid his hand slowly down her bare leg, sending shivers up to her thighs. Finally he found her foot. With an easy heave, he lifted her off the ground. She gasped slightly and balanced both hands on his strong shoulders.

"It's okay, I got you." Ward stood to his full height. She rested her hip against the strength of his shoulder and raised her arms.

"I'm feeling along the ceiling now. Everything feels the same."

"Search for a break in the tile."

"It's all tile." She ran her palms against the ceiling in frantic circles. She had to find the opening. If this didn't work, they might be stuck here for hours.

Finally one palm snagged on an irregularity. "Wait, this may be it." She pushed on the unusual tile with all her strength, but it didn't budge. Frustration made her muscles bunch. "I can't get it."

"On the count of three, I'll jump and you push. Between the two of us, we can get it open."

On three, Ward jumped and Hannah shoved her palms against the ceiling with all her force, very aware of the strong arms wrapped around her legs. Nothing.

"Let's try it again," he suggested.

"No. Outside of using my head as a battering ram, I don't think we're going to get it open. It's probably not the trap door anyway. Maybe it's just a replacement tile and that's why it felt funny."

"Okay." He loosened the hold around her legs and eased her down, along his body. A delicious friction erupted between them as she slid down, her skirt riding up. His hair-rough legs tickled her bare thighs.

Her toes touched the floor and she backpedaled in a

desperate attempt to move away from his masculine heat. He steadied her with a hand to her shoulder, searing her. She found her hands resting on the firmness of his chest. Her stomach muscles quivered at the unleashed strength of his body and she pushed herself away, her fingertips trailing along the hair of his muscled forearms.

She was acting like an idiot. Ward must think her insane. Trapped inside an elevator with a crazy person, this must be his lucky day.

WHAT WAS WRONG WITH HER all of a sudden? She obviously didn't want him to touch her. But why? He'd felt a rush of adrenaline the moment their skin made contact. He'd swear her body trembled slightly at his touch. It had been a long time since his last failed attempt at a relationship, but could he be that far off the mark? And could he be that much out of practice?

Ward rubbed the sweat off his face and slicked his hair back. That haircut he'd gotten two days ago had come in handy. Less hair, less heat. He could only imagine how hot Hannah must be. Her only concession to the growing inferno had been to remove…hell, he didn't know what she removed, but it still made him hard.

When she stood to take off whatever bit of feminine cloth she thought expendable, he realized he'd never be able to wipe the imagined scene out of his mind. His body had quickened at the rustling of material, the sound of her nails scraping on the silky fabric. He'd checked his urge to help her.

Brett would laugh his head off if he could see the two of them. His friend said he'd spotted a change in Ward. It seemed his senses finally agreed, but the woman obviously couldn't bear his touch. She seemed to be keeping herself as far away from him as she could.

Maybe that was in her best interests. His body stirred again as she sat across from him, her perfume coming to him on a puff of air. Pears and strawberry. It made him ache all the more to taste her. She possessed a delicate strength. Something that called out to some primitive instinct he had to safeguard. Where the hell had that urge come from?

It must be the strange circumstance he found himself in. It didn't make sense to get personal in a case. He saw what losing that narrow-minded focus had done to Brett's career at the Bureau. He was now stuck at a desk job in a field office in Salt Lake. That wasn't for him. No way.

Okay, so he'd been noticing her as more than just a suspect. Who wouldn't notice her auburn curls? Or that dimple in her chin she hated and her full red lips?

"Ward, we haven't tried to pry the doors apart. I think there's supposed to be some kind of catch."

"I thought of that, Hannah, but I don't want to risk it if we don't have to. We don't know where the elevator has stopped. You could break an arm or a leg dropping down. If we climb out and the electricity should come back on while we're half in, half out of the elevator—"

Hannah shuddered. "It's okay. I get the picture. How long do you think it's been? About an hour and a half?"

"About that long."

She stood and a rush of air circulated his way. "Well, I can't stand being in these clothes much longer."

He heard the zip of her skirt and whoosh as it fell to the ground. He swallowed. Hard. He heard another whoosh as what he assumed was her blouse hit the floor. If he heard another, he could only guess what that particular item of clothing would be. Images of a nearly naked Hannah standing before him made his mind go fuzzy and his body grow hard. He didn't need this rush of heat. He was hot enough already.

Thankfully, he heard no other whoosh.

"Umm. That's better. This elevator wall actually feels cool against my skin."

Ward cleared his throat and fought to find his voice. In the end, he gave up trying. A long, dark silence stretched between them.

"Ward?"

"Yes?"

"Talk to me."

"What about? Cars, movies, advancements in security technology?"

"I don't care."

He'd been making a joke, but the steely vulnerability he'd detected in her voice stopped him from making another attempt at humor. She was reaching out to him, and he knew that was unusual for her because he shared the same symptoms. She reached out, but didn't like the needing to.

Damn, Brett was right. He rubbed his leg and smiled at the irony of it. He was going to have a heck of a time proving this one innocent. Ward couldn't see her as a true criminal.

And yet, Hannah was his number-one suspect.

Good to see he hadn't lost his ability in finding the surest method of driving a woman away.

4

"So, HOW LONG HAVE YOU lived in Gallem?" Ward asked.

Hannah tried not to fall into full-blown panic. It was just a question. A casual question normal people asked other completely normal people every day.

All she had to do was answer it like a normal person.

Ah, and there was the problem.

"I, uh—"

She took a deep, calming breath. *Hannah Garrett* knew her story backward and forward. Sideways even.

"A little over a year," she told him. Excellent. No stutter. No hesitation. It's not as if she hadn't given out this exact same memorized information a dozen times before. So why was she tongue-tied with Ward?

"Yeah? I'm new to Gallem, too. Where did you live before?"

Okay, another normal question. A zero on the unusual scale. Ward was the security guy, of course he'd ask questions about a person's background to pass the time.

"Oh, I moved around a lot, probably the same as you did in the military."

Good. She was following procedure. When conversations grew too personal, turn the focus back onto the other person.

"Your parents didn't mind?"

"They both died when I was little. I grew up in foster care. Once you're eighteen, that's basically it."

"That's rough. I knew a few men like that in the military. They couldn't find anyone for you to live with?"

Kyle hadn't cared about her past. Only what she could give him in the present. She couldn't recall a single time he'd asked about her family. His living in the moment had been one of his appeals. Admittedly, she'd been kind of relieved, not really wanting to talk about the group home, her foster mother. Growing up, she'd felt judged her whole life. Kyle had never looked down on her. He was content to have her by his side, the perfect arm candy in a sexy dress and makeup. All that mattered to Kyle was the here and now.

Ward was different, though. She felt an odd comfort in talking about the past with Ward. Since Kyle hadn't known her origins, she'd opted to keep her real history with this latest identity.

"Hannah, if you don't want to talk about—"

"No, it's okay. Actually, there could be a whole slew of relatives out there that I don't know about. The father's name on my birth certificate was left blank. I was told I lived with my mother until I was three, but I don't remember her. She just dropped me off at the daycare center, and never came back."

"That's rough."

"She was only sixteen when she had me. Maybe she

thought leaving me would give me a chance to have a better life. At least that's how I like to think of it."

"I bet you're right."

She smiled in the darkness. Ward agreeing with her was practically erotic. Most people would probably flash her their most skeptical look at her fanciful need to think well of a mother who had abandoned her.

Ward's sympathy, and more, for her, threw her off-kilter for a moment. Her purse still lay beside her, so she grabbed it, sinking her hand down to the depths. Anything to distract her.

"Hey, I think I found a package of mints at the bottom of my purse. Feels like three of them," Hannah said, rummaging in the darkness.

"I'll give you a thousand dollars for them," Ward said.

Hannah laughed. She hadn't laughed in so long, her laughter sounded a little rusty even to her own ears.

He had the sexiest voice she'd ever heard in her life. Of course she'd been listening to nothing but that rich, deep baritone of his for the last few hours. She'd read that when someone lost one sense, the others became more acute.

She believed it now.

Her ears had become especially sensitive to his voice as it wrapped around her, surrounding her like a sensual fog.

"So, what brought you to Gallem?" she asked, suddenly needing to turn the focus of their conversation away from her life.

Ward had been with the FBI long enough to know

when someone was trying to divert his attention. Not a smooth transition, but the way Hannah phrased her question would make his refusal to answer seem rude.

"Things had gotten a little stale. A friend told me I needed to get into life. When I saw the job at P&L I applied. I didn't know Gallem was so hot."

She laughed. He loved a woman's laugh.

The fanning motion across from him stopped for a moment, then resumed. "So have you been more satisfied with your life since moving here?"

Here it was. His opportunity to open up. Share. He cleared his throat. He had an urge to say something glib, to pass his earlier statement off as a joke. But something in her voice, a hesitation before asking, perhaps a similar resignation, he didn't know, but he sensed a kindred spirit. He and Hannah had both turned their backs on life.

Maybe being stuck in an elevator wasn't such bad luck at all. Maybe it was Murphy's way of giving him a wake-up call. But what could he say? He'd been undercover for most of his adult life. It was hard to know the difference between reality and make-believe. "My parents died when I was seventeen."

"Mmm."

The sound, almost a hum, didn't really mean anything, but it was oddly comforting. An invitation to continue.

There was no need to close his eyes, his usual habit when thoughts of that day threatened to return. But it wouldn't help. It wouldn't be any darker than the elevator, and it wouldn't block the picture of his mother and father dead on the living room floor. "They were murdered."

"So that's why you went into law enforcement."

His throat clenched, then he swallowed. For a moment, he thought she'd guessed his true reason for being here. Then he realized she spoke of his security job.

"Go on," she urged.

Goose bumps formed on his skin despite the heat. "I had a life of football games and an after-school job. After that I went on a mission to solve the murder."

"The police let you?"

The images pounded his brain fast and furious. "They couldn't hold me back at first. Then one of the cops, one of those bristly old-school guys took me aside. Told me I was hampering rather than helping. He told me to finish school; my parents wanted better for me. Of course he didn't say it so nicely. I took my GED and entered the Marines."

For a moment, he desperately wanted to do what he always did when someone attempted to get close to him. He wanted to move away, to close down. Despite the wall of untruths between them, he knew something was mounting. And he knew Hannah understood it, too.

He wanted her. Ward wanted her so badly he almost reached for her.

"Do you think we could pass out in here?" she asked. "It's getting so hot."

He sighed again. There it was again, that subtle vulnerability. A different kind of frustration built inside him. An urge to shelter her. Not that she'd appreciate it much. In his brief experience, she clearly took pride in her ability to take care of herself and likely wouldn't want his unexpected need to protect.

Which didn't jive with being a thief. Had she been blackmailed? What were the secrets she so desperately tried to hide? He had to get her to be honest about her involvement in the money laundering. Try to make her trust him. Her body already did…to a point. Then, once she'd confessed, he'd find her a lawyer. He'd make sure the AG's office went easy on her. Maybe they'd even swing full immunity.

Earlier she'd asked him to talk to her. Maybe it was time to learn a few of her secrets. The wafts of air around him told him she was fanning herself. He'd glean more if she sat there scared about passing out in this hot box. The possibility was there. But remote if Brett got on the stick.

Despite his frustration, he knew he owed her more, and decided to relieve her tension. "They'll find us soon. Brett will pull through."

Everything about his voice offered comfort. Understanding. The luring temptation of letting her guard down once. Just once.

She shivered, her shoulder bumping the wall of the elevator.

"Did you finally get cooler?" he asked.

"Uh…yes." She certainly didn't want him to know how he affected her. "Hard to believe after all this heat, huh? Trouble is…I can't find my blouse." *Not bad for an excuse right off the cuff.*

Hannah shifted to her knees and began patting the floor, feeling for her clothes.

She heard Ward move. Felt the air shift as his big body moved. "Here, I'll help."

His fingers searched beside hers. Ward's hand sent a zip of air along her leg, creating goose bumps on her calf. She gasped when his finger grazed her knee. Thank goodness he couldn't see her skin. She knew she'd be flushed. If the lights came on, she'd have a lot of explaining to do.

"Sorry," he said, his voice strangely tight.

"No problem."

"Seems the only thing I'm finding are my own clothes and you," Ward said.

Perhaps making light of the situation would make it less charged. "It's hard to know what you're feeling in here, it's so dark."

A chuckle, from deep in his chest, filled the small compartment. "Oh, believe me, I know what I'm touching."

A shot of pure desire raced through her. She quickly returned to patting the floor. She needed that blouse now for more than the ruse of being chilled. She needed a barrier, a protection against the potent, sexual promise of Ward Coleman. And her own need to be very, very naughty.

Their fingers entwined as they found her blouse at the same time. She expected him to drop his hand, to apologize, to move away from her. All his other touches had been accidents.

But not this one.

Ward trailed his hand up her arm to rest at her shoulder. Shivers emanated from his caressing fingers and spread throughout her body, like a stone disturbing a still lake.

Everything about him unsettled her.

But he moved his hand no farther. She understood why. He was giving her the chance to pull away. She'd only been in close contact with him for so little time, but already she knew how tender his strength could be. She knew how much in tune he was to her. She knew how much she wanted him.

Hannah didn't move away.

But she could do nothing more than that. She hadn't purposely touched another human being in a sexual manner in four years. Hadn't allowed another to touch her.

But here, it was dark.

Ward would never see her body. Never see what she had to hide. The dark had become her favorite companion, her comfort. Now the dark would give her something else. A chance to feel, if only briefly, like a woman again.

She didn't pull away, and with a sigh she leaned against him.

Ward groaned and tugged her to him tightly. They knelt together on the floor of the elevator, touching from thigh to chest. She burned with wanting. Ward's hands left her shoulders and slid their way to her chin.

Her heart stopped beating. Her lungs refused to make the necessary moves to suck in air. Every function in her body stilled. Waited. Then Ward's lips covered hers.

Firm. Heated. Sensual.

She didn't know what she'd expected, perhaps a tentative brushing of lips, or a questioning kind of kiss between two near-strangers. But she wasn't prepared for the sure, confident way his mouth found hers.

Amazing lips. The man possessed amazing lips. Firm and soft, his mouth moved gently along hers. Just a muted caress that promised really big things to come.

The heat, the utter silence around the elevator car, her thirst faded. Nothing but this kiss mattered right now. Nothing but just a moment away from everything to experience this man.

Ward's lips continued to move across hers, drawing a response.

And just when she was about to give it to him, his mouth left hers. His lips traveled across her cheek, above her brows, down to her chin. The warmth of his breath a sensuous caress to her skin. Then once more his lips found hers.

She finally breathed. Breathed in Ward. He sucked in her bottom lip, and her mouth began to tingle. It had been so long. So long since she'd felt wanted and desired as a woman. So long since she wanted to touch. Taste. Explore a man's body. And she wanted to do all those things with Ward.

The erotic touch of his tongue to the sensitive skin of her bottom lip, the gentle touch of his teeth sent her into action. She didn't want to just feel, she wanted to give the caresses.

She wound her arms around his neck, urging him closer. He sank his fingers into the length of her hair, shifting her head in line with his. His mouth widened, and with a small cry, she opened her mouth to his searching tongue.

His fingers trailed from her hands, up her arms, then paused at her shoulders. He drew her to him. A seductive invitation.

One she took. Hannah wrapped her arms around his back. The suddenness of her move knocked Ward off balance. He toppled, falling onto his discarded clothes, twisting so that she fell on top of him.

She would have lost herself entirely in the excitement of his kiss had it not been for the distraction of his muscled chest. Or the tightness of his belly against the rounded softness of hers. Or the hair on his hard legs tickling the bare tenderness of her inner thighs as she straddled his hips. Hannah felt, in thrilling detail, how much he wanted her.

Hannah rocked an inch forward. Ward groaned. "Hannah, do that again."

She arched her head back, letting her long hair flow down her back. Then gave another experimental rock. Then another. The darkness, her dear friend, made her bold. Her movement caused a delicious friction. Ward groaned again.

Sitting on her heels, her fingers tingled with indecision. Hannah wanted to touch him from head to toe. Where to touch first? There were so many tantalizing places to drive a man wild with wanting.

She raked her fingers from his smooth shoulders down his hairy chest to the flatness of his stomach. Her fingers met the barrier of boxers. *Ahh,* he'd left them on. She loved a man in boxers.

She wanted to kiss him, taste him. She bent and found the sensitive hollow below his ear.

His deep chuckle reverberated around their confines. "Why did we spend all that time talking?"

Suddenly Hannah wanted to laugh. She'd not felt this free, not since...

No! Don't think about it. Don't let that intrude here, in the one place where she could hide from the truth. She twined her fingers in his hair and pulled his lips closer to hers. "Seems to me you're the one doing the talking right now."

She felt his smile against her lips. "Easily remedied." He lifted his lips the fraction that separated them. She opened her mouth hungrily.

Tracing her tongue along the path her fingers had taken only moments before, she soon found her mouth at the barrier of the band.

Ward's fingers stopped her progress, moving her higher. "Do that and it'll be over before it's begun."

Hannah wanted to laugh out loud with pleasure. With sexual power. It had been so long since she'd had this kind of power with a man. To feel utterly desirable. To make a man think he'd die if he didn't have her. Right. Then.

She was the seductress. A forbidden role. Except now. In the dark.

With a smile she knew he couldn't see, Hannah stood and moved out of his reach.

"Where are you?" His voice, tight with need, quickened the beat of her heart.

"Feel your way," she told him. Once again the seductive tease.

He surged toward her, his body dragging along hers. Ward pushed her gently against the cold wall of the elevator. She welcomed the coolness against her flushed skin, but the chill lasted only a moment. Ward made every inch of her body hot.

In the darkness she sensed him towering over her, big and strong. Close, yet barely touching. The hair on his chest tickled and tantalized the tips of her nipples through her bra.

"Touch me," she told him, desire she had no wish to hide lacing her words.

"Oh, I will," he groaned against the sensitive skin of her neck.

His warm tongue teased the sensitive skin below her ear. She sucked in her breath and held it as sensation after incredible sensation washed over her, cleansing her of her thoughts of the past. Hannah dug her fingers into his hair, pushing him away then pulling him close once more.

As if he couldn't stay away from her mouth for long, his lips landed on hers. But this was no gentle soft kiss from before. This was a determined and concentrated strike on her senses. It was a kiss meant to elicit a carnal response.

And it did. Her skin grew heated. Her nipples tightened. The soft flesh between her legs grew warm and wet. Her knees began to buckle and she began to slide down.

Ward pressed himself against her, and she felt his erection. Hard and growing even bigger against her body.

Propping her against the wall of the elevator, he bent and traced the outer edge of her bra with his tongue. Then he teased her nipple, the thin cotton fabric the only separation between his lips and her heated skin.

With a moan, she arched her back. Despite the barrier of her bra, red-hot desire raced from her nipple to between her legs. He trailed his hand up her legs until he reached the material of her panties.

Serviceable cotton, not the silky nothings or wispy thongs from her past. Thank God for the dark, but then by the tender desperation of his fingers, Ward's only concern about her panties was whether they would come off. Not whether they were sexy enticements.

The soft flesh between her thighs tingled. "Please, I…"

"Please what?" Ward asked, his voice husky and tight with strain. He felt this same burning need she did.

"Keep making me feel this way."

He nudged her thighs. Hannah gasped. It could have been only a moment or many minutes she stood against the wall waiting for his next move, she just didn't know. This was not her usual style. In the past, she'd been the seductress, the one in control. With barely a touch through her panties, her body quaked at the hint of his caresses to come. She lost all thought, all control and only felt.

Her ragged breathing filled the cramped elevator compartment.

Ward groaned into the hollow between her breasts. "I want to make love to you."

Make love. Make love? His choice of words forced strength to her legs. She didn't want love. Taking a deep breath, she forced her trembling muscles to regain control.

What the hell was she doing? She'd known the man less than two weeks, most of that time filled with suspicion.

Except she knew the hard planes of his body. Somehow she'd managed to catalog every expression on his face. Now she knew the taste of him. Ironic, but she'd never realized she knew Ward better than the face she'd seen in the mirror for the last four years.

Her hands curled around his shoulders to push him away, but stopped. Somewhere, from far off, she registered an odd clanging.

"Did you hear that?" he asked.

5

ANOTHER CLANGING SOUND echoed up toward them.

"I definitely heard that." Hannah's spirits soared with the sound. Help had obviously arrived. They were saved.

Ward stood and pounded on the floor with his feet. "Hey, we're here, we're stuck in the elevator."

"Is there a Ward Coleman up there?"

"Yes, and there's another passenger in here with me, Hannah Garrett."

"You folks just sit tight. We'll be right there to get you."

Was she ready for their brief time together to end? Here, in the darkness, she'd transformed, however briefly, into a woman of mystery rather than one of secrets. In the elevator she could forget. Forget about her past. Forget how her skin mirrored the scars on her heart.

"Once we're out, let's go…celebrate. I'll take you out for a nice dinner. And to talk."

There was a whole lot of emphasis on that word *talk*. A fresh panic, similar to her initial fears when the elevator had stopped, assailed her. She couldn't see him again. She didn't want him to see her. He threatened her. He made her want things. Things she knew she could never have.

He'd bared a part of himself. Men didn't do that often. And that threatened her even more.

Think fast. "Ward, I really would like to get cleaned up and—" A jerk of the car stopped her words.

"Won't be long now. I can't wait to take a shower."

"Hey, down there. Can you hear us?"

The voice was right outside the elevator door.

"Yes, we're here."

"The firefighters are on their way. They just secured the elevator."

Hannah gasped. "Ward, I don't have my blouse on." Or her skirt for that matter. She dropped to her knees, groping along the floor for her clothes. The material under her fingers only felt like his stuff. With rising desperation, she tugged him down beside her. "Help me. I must look awful."

"You've been trapped in a sweltering elevator for a couple of hours. No one expects you to look good. In fact, it might be a good idea if we went over to the hospital and had some IV fluids. We're likely bordering on dehydration."

"Ward, they're about to open those doors and I'm only in my bra and panties. Heat or no heat, I don't want anyone to find me like that. Here, give me your phone, maybe the lights can help us find our clothes."

With a punch to the keys, Ward's phone buzzed and a dull, greenish light illuminated a tiny patch on the floor. After hours of complete darkness, even that amount of light hurt her eyes and made her blink.

Her skirt lay bunched up in the corner. She grabbed the material, and with hurried, awkward movements yanked it on. She almost didn't care if she found her blouse, just as long as the concealing folds of her skirt were in place.

Beside her, Ward tugged on his shorts. She went back to her searching.

The feel of soft, cottony fabric engulfed her shoulders. "Here, wear my shirt."

The folds of the material held his masculine scent of wood and chypre, and a flood of warmth snaked through her body.

Several more voices streamed through the elevator doors. Her fingers fluttered as she shoved her arms through the sleeves of his shirt. Overcome with a sudden urge to hold on to their time in the dark together, she turned to him. "Ward, I—"

"Ward, is that you?"

Beside her he chuckled, followed by a full-bodied laugh of happiness. "Brett? I knew you'd come through for me, buddy."

She had the feeling he didn't laugh very often. She swallowed back a sob. It was almost over. A grinding sound drew her attention to the thin space between the doors. A small stream of light poked through as a wrench wedged its way into the elevator.

She turned away, the light blinding her eyes.

"You're stuck between floors. We've secured the car and once we have the doors apart and locked in place, we'll pull you up and out."

Hannah pressed herself against the far wall of the

elevator. Mortified, she wanted to disappear. Would it be obvious what they'd done to pass the time? With an awkward grinding noise, someone pushed the doors fully open and secured them with a long, metal rod.

Although blinking furiously at the bright light, she couldn't help glancing toward Ward.

He turned and smiled at her and the warmth from his eyes penetrated the darkness surrounding her heart. For just one moment, hope filled her. How nice it would be to pretend she were normal. His green eyes burned with heat and promise. She could only stare into his eyes, not ready to face the reality.

"You ready to get out?"

Hannah broke the contact and looked to where the voice had come from. Two strong arms reached down from the floor above. She couldn't back up against the wall anymore.

"Hannah, you go first," Ward urged.

Her throat constricted and she couldn't speak. She simply shook her head.

With a hurried step, he walked toward her and took her hand. He gave her a quick, hard kiss on the mouth. "I'll pull you up then. I'll be waiting for you on the other side."

Ward kissed her again then turned. He grabbed the two hands, which then hoisted him up and out of the elevator. She stood alone.

It was her turn.

She heard Brett welcoming him.

One of the hands beckoned her. "You ready, lady?"

She took a breath and broke into a rueful smile. *Acknowledge the fear, but don't give in to it.* She stepped from the shadows and into the light, grabbing both hands.

"Ward, what in the world did you do with yourself all this time?" she heard Brett ask.

She emerged from the elevator, blinking furiously from the last bit of daylight streaming through the lobby windows and from the large portable emergency lights stationed around the elevator.

"Oh. I see."

Ward rushed to her, his bare feet masking his approach. With a tender hand, he smoothed her hair from her face. She held back her urge to pull away. "Told you we'd make it."

Her shoulders slumped and she leaned into Ward's hand, which was gently stroking her forehead. "I—"

One of the EMTs efficiently barged between them. He handed her a bottle of water and a cold compress. Hannah couldn't decide which felt better. Both were bliss.

She looked over to Ward who was receiving the same treatment. Brett talked to him, but his gaze kept shifting over to her. He smiled, and she couldn't help but smile back. Maybe she could still pull this off. Maybe she could spend a bit more time with Ward. If only for a little while. Then she remembered Kyle.

Guilt stabbed at her. Unwanted memories flashed, and she squeezed her eyes shut. What business did she have even thinking about grabbing a few minutes of happiness? Not when she could be putting not just her own life in jeopardy, but someone else's, too. For just a short time, Ward had made her forget the guilt, and forgetting was deadly.

Ward's laugh stretched across the distance between them, and she opened her eyes. He had a great laugh. She watched as he said something to the tech taking his temperature with an ear gauge, and then walked to her. "We'll have to use the stairs going down, but it won't be too bad. We were stuck between the fifth and sixth floors."

Hannah looked behind her. The workers had propped open the outer doors of the elevator with several steel poles. They'd only had a foot and a half space of clearance between the bottom of the sixth floor and the top of the elevator. An orange mesh barrier blocked the remaining gap of the shaft. Ward had been right not to attempt an escape that way until they were truly desperate.

"You remember Brett?"

"Nice to see you again, Hannah," Brett said. With his Stetson, boots and jeans, he looked dressed for a night on the town, country style. She gave him as much of a smile as she could, but she had to get out of there. Someone had finally switched off the mega-kilowatt emergency lights, but the fading sunlight still pierced her eyes. All the people buzzing around increased the tension in her neck with each pass.

Ward led her toward the stairwell. "You'll feel better once we get outside and there's a breeze."

She stumbled on the first step down and Ward grabbed her under the arm to steady her. "I'm okay, really." And she took another step to prove it, but he didn't release his grip.

Thankfully he moved in front of her so he couldn't see how nervous she felt. She'd become an expert at hiding her emotions and feelings, but after what had happened with Ward in the elevator, she felt too raw, too exposed. She watched his dark blond head, memorizing every strand. Occasionally he would turn around and smile. But each step was agony. Once they reached outside, she knew what she'd have to do.

Flee.

Then another step. Maybe Kyle would be recaptured. Maybe she could stay.

Another step. No, with his job, Ward wouldn't be able to leave the mysteries of her past alone.

Leaving was her only option. Again.

How could this be? How could the thought of leaving someone she'd known such a short time cause her this much pain?

They rounded the last corner and made their way into the lobby. She committed everything from the potted plants to the tasteful artwork on the walls to memory. Here would be her last moments with Ward.

One of the firefighters handed over her purse. She thanked him and Ward led her aside. "Forget about a big dinner. Let's order pizza, and we can go back to your place or mine."

"Let me take a rain check. I just want a shower and then some sleep."

"The EMTs want us to go to General and check us out for dehydration."

She injected a ring of normalcy into her voice. "No, it's okay. I feel fine." She tried to break free, but he wouldn't let her.

"At least let me drive you home."

She shook her head. "My car's here. I'd be stuck the rest of the weekend without it."

Ward reached into his back pocket and pulled out his wallet. "Here's my card. My pager number is on there and I'll write down my home phone number. Call me when you wake up."

She didn't reach for it.

He must have finally sensed her hesitation was due to more than just the aftermath of their rescue. "You're not giving me the brush-off?"

Hannah tried to laugh, but it rang hollow and brittle to even her own ears. "Let's not do this here."

The casual expression he wore faded. "When?"

A ringing buzz echoed through her head. *No ties. No promises. No emotions.* That's what she'd vowed all those years ago. Why couldn't Ward be like any other man?

"Please, Ward, let's just get out of here. I'll call you tomorrow."

His face was a picture of tension and doubt that almost unnerved her. She turned and he let her go. Relieved, she quickened her steps through the revolving door.

As promised, outside a cool breeze ruffled her hair. She closed her eyes and took a deep, calming breath.

She wasn't prepared for a rush of footsteps.

"Are you one of the people rescued from the elevator? What was it like trapped in there for hour after hour?"

A paramedic cursed behind her. "I hate it when reporters scan the police radio."

A cameraman from one of the four local TV stations

aimed his camera right at her. The pretty blond reporter was jotting down notes in a spiral notepad.

Then Ward's strong arm blocked her from the camera and reporters. He ushered her away, but the reporter and cameraman followed. Her stomach roiled. Ward had shielded her, but was it in time? Pictures. *Oh, no.* Pictures of her.

She'd be found.

Hannah pushed against Ward and made a run back into the building. A firefighter prevented anyone following her. Grabbing a flashlight left behind, by the emergency worker. She raced to the stairwell that led to the parking garage.

Taking the steps two at a time, her hands skimmed the handrail. She slipped into the darkness of the garage with ease. She only spotted three cars with the beam from the flashlight, which made locating her own car easier. Sometimes she had difficulty remembering where she'd left her car from her habit of never parking in the same place twice.

Opening her purse, she felt among the lipstick, pocketbook and day planner for her keys. She touched the cool sharpness of the metal and pulled them out, running toward her car, pushing the automatic unlock button with all her strength.

The lock opened with a click and the internal light shot on.

Her tires squealed as she looped her way through the empty garage to the exit. On the street, she spared a glance in her rearview mirror. No one followed. She sighed with relief.

She sped down the streets, Ward, the emergency workers and the reporter becoming a tiny blur.

The sun set behind her in the west as she drove to her apartment on autopilot. She blasted herself with the car's air-conditioning until a welcome chill settled over her skin.

The reporter had upped the ante. She'd been worried enough with just having to contend with Ward. But if there were pictures...*he* could find her.

She'd have to leave. There was no question about it, even if they caught Kyle and returned him to prison. It wouldn't be hard. She'd started over before. First she'd left what little security she'd managed to make for herself. The next time she'd just abandoned stuff. Now she'd be leaving a piece of her heart.

Hannah crossed her fingers hoping that no traffic cops dwelled in the downtown area as she made just-this-side-of-legal stops at the stop signs. The street-lights flickered, casting a yellow glow indicating the boundaries of the controlled blackout area. Very little traffic lingered on the road. She lurched into a parking space in front of her apartment and dashed up the stairs, letting herself in.

Scanning the room containing her possessions, she frowned. She'd be leaving a lot more than her heart. That was ridiculous. Could she fall for a stranger in a few hours? No. The idea was preposterous.

She shook off the silly idea and headed toward the telephone in the kitchen and pressed the speed dial setting. In a moment, she was connected to her emergency contact who wasted no time on pleasantries like saying hello.

"I've been compromised," Hannah said.

"You sure?"

"One hundred percent. I was caught outside my office building by a reporter. There was a camera."

"Shit. At least the safe house is ready. Someone will pick you up in fifteen minutes. You know the drill."

Yeah, she knew the drill. "What about Kyle? Have they found him?"

"A few unconfirmed sightings, but the subject is still on the loose."

She replaced the receiver and forced herself not to shake. Even if Kyle was free, he was at least three states away. She'd have time to pack.

Hannah looked around her tiny efficiency with a critical eye. There were few things she wanted to take with her. She'd miss her yellow stars and black walls. Perhaps she'd paint the new place the same way. Kicking off her shoes, she hurried to the bedroom. She pulled the plug on her air mattress. She'd hate to leave that behind.

She'd need to pack a few toiletries. In her last retreat she'd forgotten some essentials and a man had to be sent out to buy some. He'd come back red-faced with few of the correct items. She grabbed a plastic sack and scooped in toothpaste, makeup and the supplies for her contacts. She twisted the ends into a knot and tossed the sack onto the deflating mattress.

Glancing once more around the bathroom, she turned off the light and headed back into the sparsely furnished bedroom. She'd love to hear what her counselor would say about the place. She smiled despite her frazzled state. She'd make an excellent case study for a shrink. The only mirror in her apartment was in the bathroom above the sink. A necessity for flossing her teeth. She'd once longed to be in front of the camera. A long time ago.

She pulled down a suitcase and placed it onto the mattress. Air blasted out of the spigot. She'd stuff in as many clothes and shoes as she could. The landlord could sell what she left behind to make up for her skipping town so quickly. Hopefully she'd be assigned somewhere with the same kind of weather. Well, maybe not *as* hot.

Mentally checking off what she needed to do, she sealed her suitcase, eyeing her work. Most everything she'd truly need was in the sack and the suitcase. She could roll any remaining things into the mattress and stuff it into a trash bag.

She'd hate to leave her job. And damn, she'd have to think of a new name. She actually liked Hannah. She'd be a horrible new parent, coming up with names. At least she never had to stick with one too long.

Hannah opened the dresser drawer and grabbed a handful of the slips she wore. She'd almost forgotten those.

With a sob, she brought the material to her chest and sat on the bed. Images of removing her slip and nearly making lo—having sex with Ward filled her mind.

Stop thinking of him. It's not solving anything.

They'd be coming for her any moment, and the last thing she needed was for them to see her all emotional. Then she'd have to stay in the safe house longer.

Only one last task remained. Racing to the kitchen,

Hannah scooted a chair under the hanging basket containing an airplane plant. The first green thing she'd managed to keep alive for some time. *Oh, well.* She uprooted the plant spilling dark soil at her feet. She pulled a sealed package from under the dirt, wiping the plastic clean. She opened the package, and for a few brief precious moments, leafed through the documents that made up Hannah Garrett.

She hopped off the chair, opened the cabinet drawer containing the shredder and began feeding the documents into the grinding metal tines.

"Now doesn't this look innocent?"

Hannah gasped and turned to see Ward standing at the front door of her apartment. The formerly locked front door. "How did you get in?"

Ward only shrugged, his face outlined from the light of the yellow security bulb on the porch.

His very angry face.

Ward obviously hadn't had a shower yet. He still wore the same shorts with the addition of an obviously borrowed Gallem Fire Department T-shirt. She'd left with his. He looked haggard, tired and frustrated.

He also looked damned good.

He closed the door behind him with a shove of his foot. "You want to tell me who the hell Hannah Garret is? And why I get a red flag when I run her name in the computer?"

"How did you find me? And why?"

"Fool that I am, I was worried. You might be in shock, so I did the only thing I could think of. The address you had on file with P&L puts you somewhere in the middle of Lake Gaylon. Luckily the DMV had this address."

"Oh. How are you able to check DMV records?"

His expression guarded, he stalked toward her.

Hannah looked down at the paper she was just about to shred. The grinding of the machine still whirled in the air. *What to do?* Her training hadn't prepared her for a lover storming into her apartment as she tried to make an escape. She bit back an inappropriate bubble of laughter. No, she didn't know exactly what to do, but she felt strongly that laughing at this moment would not be the correct choice.

"What do you want?" she asked.

"Why don't you start by telling me who you really are and why you ran away?"

The phone rang once. They both looked at it. Silence stretched between them. Then the telephone rang two more times.

"Ahh. That sounds suspiciously like a signal." Ward walked into the kitchen, fully blocking any escape. The skin along his cheeks stretched taut. Any trace of the tender lover with promise in his eyes had vanished.

She fed the last piece of paper into the machine and Ward charged for her, grabbing her arm and yanking her to her feet. "Great, all the evidence is gone. To think I was beginning to discount you as a suspect."

"Suspect? Of what?"

"I'm on to you, and what's going on at P&L." He pulled her toward the window, thrust the curtains aside and waved. "Let's just see if we can attract the attention of your friend."

Fear for Ward's safety prompted her to pull at his arm. She fell into his body, her collarbone hitting something hard at his shoulder. The unmistakable outline of a gun.

6

HAD WARD COME HERE to kill her after all? But why now?

A slow anger burned in her heart. They could do what they wanted to her, but Hannah wouldn't let him get her contact, not if she could help it. One person had died on her behalf already. She couldn't bear the thought of another person losing their life because of her. Wrenching free of his hold, she threw her shoulder into Ward's legs, the momentum of her fall knocking him to his knees.

He grabbed at her shoulders for balance, pulling her backward with him. She scrambled to her knees, trying to get away. His arm shot out, snaking around her ankle. She fell against his side and he groaned, but his fingers tied her to him like a steel clamp.

Lying against him chest to chest, she patted him down, searching for the gun she'd felt earlier. If she could get it, she'd be safe. Turn the tables on him. Force him into the bathroom and barricade the door. Then she could make her escape.

Ward seized her fingers, spun her onto her back and pinned her to the carpeted floor. The nylon of the old shag tickled the back of her neck.

The sound of their labored breathing filled the air. He locked his green gaze to hers. Now would be the time. He'd kill her now. She scrunched her eyes tight. *Think. Think.*

"Why?" he asked.

The emotion behind that one word cut to her soul. She opened her eyes and met his again. They were filled with anger, but not of the killing kind. Despite the fact he held her pinned to the floor, her fear started to lessen. He could have killed her a dozen times. But he hadn't.

He'd said something about P&L? Just what was going on?

Ward must have sensed the change in her because he loosened his grip and the anger in his eyes softened.

The sound of boots on the steps outside her apartment door made them both start. "Now would be a good time to share those secrets, Hannah."

She had to protect him. "Just do what they say, Ward. Please. And you won't get hurt."

"What?" he asked, sounding completely bewildered.

With a quick kick, the front door flew off its hinges. Two men, armed with guns, entered.

"Any others?"

Hannah recognized the voice as her contact on the telephone. Jernigan. She'd been with him before.

"Hannah. Any others with him?"

She shook her head. "Just him. He's got a gun."

The other man pulled a very resisting Ward off her. "Don't hurt him," she pleaded. And Ward stopped his struggles.

She gasped when the officer threw Ward against the wall. The force sent a few star stickers floating down to the floor. He propped Ward's arms apart and kicked his legs wide with his booted foot.

"You have the right to remain silent. You—"

"I know the drill. I'm with the FBI."

"What?" She and Jernigan asked the question at the same time.

"ID's in the back pocket."

One of the officers trained his gun on Ward's back while the other reached into his pocket. He found the black leather holder where Ward said it would be and flipped it open. The light bounced off the gold of the badge as he showed it to them.

"You can turn around. Uh, sorry. I'm Waverly. That's Jernigan."

Ward turned and nodded. He replaced the badge in his back pocket.

"What's your interest in Ms. Garrett?" Jernigan demanded.

"She's a suspect."

"That's ridiculous. In what?" Hannah asked, confused anger replacing her relief.

"Hannah wouldn't do anything wrong," Waverly said, his tone defensive.

"Care to elaborate?" Jernigan asked, showing no signs of agitation.

"No."

Jernigan leaned forward. "I can assure you Ms. Garrett is not a criminal."

Ward shrugged. "Not good enough. When I found

her this evening, she was shredding papers, packed and ready to flee."

"What's going on here?" Hannah asked.

"I don't know, but we don't have time to find out. Grab your stuff and let's go," Jernigan told her. "Where's the shredder?"

"In the kitchen." Waverly dashed to the kitchen where he grabbed the paper out of the basket below the shredding device. He tossed the scraps into the sink where he set them on fire. After a few moments, he doused the flame with a turn of the tap.

"I want some answers," Ward said.

Jernigan grabbed her mattress while Hannah reached for the plastic sacks. "Car's downstairs. Turn to the left."

"You can't take her. She's my prisoner."

Jernigan shook his head. "She's been in our custody all along. Witness Protection."

"Who the hell are you?"

"U.S. Marshals."

Ward cut a glance her way, his eyes narrowed further in suspicion. Great. In custody of the U.S. Marshals.

Ward stepped between them and the door. Hannah stood back and watched.

"You're not taking her. If you don't want the Justice Department breathing down your necks because you just stole away my prime suspect, she comes with me."

Hannah gasped. "Prime suspect for what?"

Jernigan motioned to the door. "We gotta get out of here now. All our lives are in danger the longer we wait." He pointed to Ward. "You, come with us or not. I don't care. We can straighten out jurisdiction later, but

Ms. Garrett *is* coming with us. We're not having this conversation right now."

She turned her attention to Ward. He swallowed, and she saw the cords of his neck bulge. "Lead the way," he finally bit out.

The three men turned and headed toward the door. Waverly slammed it shut, and they flanked her as she walked down the stairs.

Outside the night had settled into a hot, muggy evening. She caught the scent of burning grass, a common occurrence in the dry hot plains in which Gallem rested. The sun had finally dipped below the horizon and the moon was making its ascent. The darkness of the night enveloped her, and for the first time since this morning's call, she felt safe.

Well, not the first time. Ward's arms in the elevator had given her a measure of comfort she'd never felt before.

She glanced over at the profile of the man walking half a pace ahead of her. The muscles of his strong jaw bunched, as if he was grinding his teeth with every step. She looked down at his hands. Surprisingly, they weren't balled into fists, but drummed along his legs, as if itching to grab something. Even his footsteps looked alert.

Hannah glanced away quickly. Just a few short hours ago, his fingers had traced along her skin with the same kind of vigilant determination. A rush of urgent desire flared and she missed the last step, stumbling a bit.

Ward's large hand on her arm steadied her. She looked into his eyes and tried to convey all the turmoil and sorrow she felt at involving him in this. At having to lie. At being who she was.

She placed her hand on his, drawing energy from the strength of him. "Ward, I—"

He pulled his hand away. "Save it for your lawyer."

The marshals stopped in front of a nondescript brown sedan with dark windows. Hannah reached for the back door, typically her escorts sat up front.

"What about him?" Waverly asked.

She watched as Jernigan pulled out his cell phone. He talked for a moment, then asked something of Ward. Ward nodded. Jernigan closed the phone and popped his head through the other door. "He'll be coming with us for the moment. Hannah, you can sit up front with me, or—"

"It's okay, I'll stay in the back with Ward."

The marshal shrugged. "It's your neck."

The man in question humphed and stretched his long legs into the backseat. Hannah scooted in alongside him and Waverly closed the door behind them.

Both marshals swung into the front seat and shut the doors. Jernigan started the car and pulled into the light traffic. Obviously most people had taken the mayor's suggestion of staying indoors and off the streets during the controlled blackouts.

Hannah swiveled in her seat to look one last time at her life in Gallem. Goodbye, stars. Goodbye, moons. Goodbye, Hannah Garrett.

"We'll be dropping you off at the local police station, Cassidy."

Hannah turned her attention away from the view of her fading home. "Cassidy, who's Cassidy?"

She spotted Jernigan hiding a smile. "Your seatmate. That's the name on his badge. Did he tell you his name was something else?"

She shot Ward an accusing glance, but he never looked her way.

"You're not dropping me off anywhere. I stay with the prisoner."

"I'm not your prisoner. You attacked me. They should be dropping you off to a cell. I haven't done anything wrong."

Ward gave her a cold stare. "That remains to be seen. Tell me what's going on," he told the officers.

A passing neon sign illuminated the irritated glance Jernigan shot Waverly. "Once you have clearance, we'll let you know. Until then, it's the station," he called to Ward from the front seat.

"And let her slip away? Not happening. I'm stuck to her like glue." Ward grabbed her hand. In an instant, cold steel wrapped around her wrist. The interior of the car reverberated with the sound of the clicking catch of handcuffs seizing her. An echoing catch sounded on Ward's wrist.

At the same time, his automatic window lowered and he hurtled what she assumed to be the key to the handcuffs into the darkness of the night.

She yanked her arm, and he released her hand. "Hey, you can't do this."

For the first time since their release from the elevator he smiled at her. "Already done."

"What are we going to do?" Waverly asked.

Jernigan angled the rearview mirror to look Ward in the eye. "Pretty clever for a Feeb."

"Not too tough to pull with a couple of marshals."

Jernigan turned to Waverly. "Get your key, and unlock the cuffs."

"I didn't bring my cuffs or my key."

"What?"

"I wasn't expecting to arrest anyone tonight."

Jernigan shook his head, and returned his attention to the road. "You'll come with us for a…" He paused a moment. "A *debriefing*. And I'll be writing an incident report about this."

Ward nodded. "Fair enough."

"And you'll have to wear a blindfold to the safe house."

"Screw that."

Jernigan angled the mirror again. Ward did not waver in his hard stare. Despite the sedan's air-conditioning, the heat and tension rose.

Hannah couldn't take it anymore. She hated confrontations of any kind. "Look, it's clear he's not fronting for Kyle. If he were going to kill me, he would have done so by now."

The standoff between the two men stretched.

"I want your service revolver," Jernigan told him.

Hardness cemented his features. For a moment, Hannah thought he'd refuse. Then Ward reached under his shirt and pulled out a black gun, extending it to the front seat handle first. Waverly took it and stashed it in the glove box.

Jernigan signaled a turn onto the highway. "Let's take Hannah to her new home."

WARD DIDN'T KNOW what the hell was going on, but he planned to find out.

After escaping from the elevator, the last thing he'd expected was to be cuffed to his suspect and taken to a safe house by U.S. Marshals.

He wouldn't look at Hannah. She'd said nothing since Jernigan had agreed to take him to the safe house with them. It was probably for the best. The last thing he wanted to hear were more lies.

But that was the thing. She hadn't really lied to him at all. What had she really ever told him? Nothing. She'd told him nothing.

That's all there was between them. Nothing.

Damn if his body still didn't react to the enticing lure of hers. He'd felt some elusive draw to her from the beginning. Brett had immediately spotted the connection between them. And now they were linked again, this time by the small chain holding their wrists together. She'd had to scoot closer to him so the cuff didn't cut into the delicate flesh of her wrist. The heat of her skin nearly scorched him.

Skin he'd touched and tasted in the darkness. He still wanted her. But he'd also wanted to drag those prisoners through James's office. Both were mistakes. Mistakes he intended not to repeat.

Cuffing himself to her was a stupid idea. But he had never lost a man. Or a woman.

Hell, even after finding her shredding documents and wrestling with her on the floor for his gun, he still thought he could save her. Had practically begged to help her. He was such an idiot. And bonus, two agents got to see his weakness. Now he could be the laughing-stock of two federal agencies. Good thing Brett was heading back to Salt Lake tonight because his baby son was running a fever.

Trying to prove her innocent, Brett had said. Yeah right. She could probably teach him a few things about crime. The only people he knew who stood custody with the U.S. Marshals and needed safe houses usually danced on the fine line between right and wrong.

Except to him there was no fine line. Right was right and wrong was wrong. And from where he sat, Hannah Garrett was on the wrong side of the line.

He knew there'd been something off with her résumé. It was too perfect. Now he knew why… because Hannah Garrett wasn't real. She was make-believe.

And the woman beside him wasn't real, either.

What they'd shared in the elevator wasn't real.

Now he just had to convince his body of that.

7

Hannah tugged.

Ward tugged back.

They'd been in the wordless war of tug-the-handcuffs for the last several miles, the clink of the chain the only sound between them.

At first she'd tried to squeeze her hand through the circle of metal without him noticing. But he'd clasped the thing too tight. Even if she pulled with all her might, she doubted she could have twisted out.

So that left her with the tug-of-war.

The dark scenery passed in a blur outside her window. Her arm lay draped between them on the backseat. Her annoyance grew with each tiny displacing movement from him. She wanted her arm exactly where she'd left it.

Her first tug of the chain happened quite by accident, a simple itch. He hadn't said anything, but he rubbed the skin beneath his cuff. So Ward had sensitive skin. Tough. Maybe he should have thought about the chafing before he'd shackled himself to her. She gave another tug when she adjusted her skirt. The pretend sneeze had really jerked his arm.

Small, childish satisfactions, but hey, she took what she could get. And there was nothing else to do. The marshals spoke in quiet tones to each other. She glanced in Ward's direction. The rigidity of his back could give lessons to starch.

FBI.

The initials flashed in her mind, hard and daunting. Everything she knew about Ward was a lie. Everything he said. Everything he did. His touch was a lie. His kiss was a lie. What he'd made her feel in the elevator, and worse, outside, was a lie.

Obviously his employment at Protter and Lane was a cover.

"Is P&L under some kind of investigation?"

"When I get my information, you'll get yours."

Since entering the program, she'd sought nothing but balance. In the space of a few hours, Ward had knocked her right off the beam. Now, she fought to steady herself. She checked off the things she *did* know about him. He didn't hesitate to use any means to find out what he wanted. Her mind replayed every meeting they'd had before the fateful trap in the elevator. His intentions were all too clear now. He'd asked her questions before; when he didn't get answers, he'd tried seduction.

He also thought her some kind of lawbreaker.

Actually, being a criminal might be a welcome relief rather than running from one.

And the barest touch of his fingers made her shudder with desire.

With a disgusted hiss, Hannah angled her body away from his.

That desire was based on a lie.

The street signs drifted into green mile markers and now trees replaced the billboards. The marshals had really found some place isolated this time. Good thing she'd packed everything she needed herself. No telling where the nearest store might be.

Jernigan signaled and turned the car off the highway. The exit sign indicated they were heading toward the secluded lake district. "The safe house is just up the road another mile."

Hannah nodded and tugged again. Ward didn't tug back. Ahh, he took away all her fun.

The car slowed, and Jernigan turned it to the left. Waverly, gun in hand, stepped out, looked around, and sprinted to the gate. With a few deft twists, he sprung open the combination lock and pushed the gate open. Jernigan drove through, then waited for Waverly to lock the gate behind them.

The dirt road leading to the safe house was heavily rutted and overgrown. The towering trees and brush lining the path made navigation difficult. No one had been down this road in a long time. She could just imagine what the inside of the house looked like.

She didn't have to wait long. The overgrowth abruptly parted to reveal a white, A-frame home badly in need of repainting. The place reminded her of those prefab homes built right after the G.I.'s returned from World War II. This had been a semipopular vacation area until the rest of the world discovered what the local farmers had known for a long time. The rich soil surrounding the lake made for the easy growth of marijuana. The governor stamped out that element a few years back. Now, only broken-down homes remained.

The headlights cast a shadow on an old rope swing hanging from one of the trees inviting a child who would never come to play.

The sad house matched her mood.

Rotting wood boarded one of the front windows. The steps leading to the porch sagged in the middle and a few of the side boards had pulled from the frame. The front door was the only thing new on the place. That and three shiny locks. She could count on that with the marshals. No one would be getting into this baby.

She'd stayed in worse.

"Home, sweet home," Jernigan said as he angled the car to the side of the house. A decrepit carport stood to the side, but she could tell with a single glance how unsound it was. One sturdy car door slam and the top would probably cave in.

Ward opened his door the same time she did. Great. The tug-of-war could begin again, this time to see whose door they'd leave through. He glanced her way and she braced herself.

Then he cocked his head toward her door and scooted along the seat toward her. With quick, fumbling hands, she released her seat belt and hopped out of the car, Ward right behind her.

Jernigan cut the headlights and the darkness welcomed them. A full moon cast just enough light to lead them to the stairs. The stars twinkled brightly, the light pollution from the city too far away.

Waverly indicated they should head for the door. "We confiscated the house from a dealer several years ago. It doesn't look like much on the outside, but there are several bedrooms and a nice bathroom with a shower."

A place she planned to hit just as soon as she could. She wanted to wash all traces of Ward Whatshisname from her body. She took a step toward the stairs, only to be stopped short. She turned to see Ward's taunting smile.

"Wait up," he told her.

She took a deep breath, gave him a tight smile, then turned again to march up the sagging steps, sensing his presence close behind her.

She waited as the agents opened the three locks and swung the door open. Guns drawn, Jernigan and Waverly took off in opposite directions once they'd entered the house.

"You two head for the kitchen while we report in. It's to the left." Jernigan called.

Ward moved to switch on a lamp. She almost wished he hadn't. This room craved color. Two large black leather sofas dominated the room, bordered by black plastic end tables. The alternating tiles of black-and-white on the floor turned wavy in her peripheral vision.

After blinking several times, the second thing to catch her attention was a large painting above one of the sofas. Taking a few steps closer, she realized the darkness of the furniture was a deliberate foil to the unusual painting. She couldn't exactly call it a nude, but the woman reclining against the simple white pillows wore just enough to be considered decent. In contrast to the starkness of the pillows, her long, auburn hair brushed her bare shoulders. A thin camisole covered her breasts, the pink tips of her nipples peeking through the sheer fabric.

Her sexually confident smile was pure seduction. A woman in control of what took place in the bedroom. Hannah couldn't take her eyes away from the painting, and an unwelcome, familiar yearning took root. For a few hours, Ward had returned to her that gift, that sexual power, and she had reveled in it.

In control? What was she thinking? She hadn't been in control of anything in four years. More if she counted her life in foster care.

And with Kyle.

"I imagine that's how you'd look waiting for your lover. Waiting for me," Ward whispered into her ear.

The heat of his body forced her body to remember things. To want things. She tamped down those desires.

"You're not my lover."

Ward's near-silent chuckle was his only response. He was trying to knock her out of her comfort zone, to rile her. That was when a person made careless statements.

Waverly barged back into the room, flipping on the overhead light. "All clear. Ahh, I see you found the painting. Our drug dealer had a unique sense of style and was an amateur painter. We're sorry, Hannah. We tried to take it down, but there's a large safe built behind it and we need to keep that for security. I could throw a sheet over it."

"No, it's okay." She turned and looked at Ward. "It's just a painting. It doesn't mean anything."

Jernigan stepped into the room. "There's a table in the kitchen. We'll debrief there."

Hannah turned to follow him, but was caught short by the chain once again. She stopped to look at Waverly, Ward nearly bumping into her. "What are we going to do about this?"

The young agent looked at Ward. Then he shifted his focus to Hannah, giving her a slight smile. "I have just the thing in the car. I'll be right back."

"Good. I don't want to be linked to this one longer than I have to."

Waverly cast a narrowed glance at Ward. "Don't worry, Hannah. You won't."

Ward laughed. "How sweet. I see you've worked your Garrett charm on him. If that's really your name."

"Come on." Hannah yanked the chain and marched toward the kitchen.

The bright yellowish light from the ancient fixture in the kitchen left few shadows. Somehow this room had escaped the decorating touch of the remodeling drug dealer. It held a certain garage-sale-find charm with a chrome table flanked by four mismatched chrome chairs, each with a different vinyl seat cover.

Someone had carefully stenciled leaves on the white painted cabinets. The varying shades of green reminded her of the foliage around Gallem at spring-time. A worn but clean, red-and-white checkered curtain hid the window. A few mismatched appliances were scattered on the countertops. Red woven rugs lay before a back door, inviting entrants to brush off their feet and stay awhile.

Inviting all but Ward.

Jernigan pulled a chair for her and she sat. Ward straddled the chair beside her. Their hands, held by the chain, lay prone between them on the silver tabletop. Jernigan eyed the chain as he took his seat, his annoyance clearly visible.

Waverly bounded in carrying bolt cutters. When Ward saw the tool he surged to his feet, hauling her up, too.

"No."

He said only one word, but the force and determination behind the single syllable tolled a struggle to come. Jernigan leaned back in his seat, the front two chair legs rising off the floor. His eyes raked Ward, assessing him.

"She made a grab for my gun. I don't want her free."

Hannah yanked on his arm, getting his attention, and glared at him. "I thought you were trying to kill me."

Ward blanched, a look of pure surprise molded his features. "Kill you? We'd almost made l— I wasn't trying to kill you."

She lifted her hands with the effort to try and make him understand. "I know that. Now. But I was scared at the time."

His earlier air of aloofness evaporated. "What did I do to make you afraid of me?"

Hannah turned away, wrapping her free arm around her waist. Did hurt lace his words?

His fingers touched her thumb then pulled her cuffed hand into his, forcing her attention back to him. Her hand tingled where their skin met.

"What kind of crime were you involved in before you got into the program?" he asked.

His question tore at her heart.

"I…uh…" The words wouldn't come. She'd pushed the past so far back into her memory that now she couldn't summon even one small explanation.

His thumb stroked her skin. "Tell me."

She knew his game now. That gentle caress of her skin. Seduction to get what he wanted. Hannah shook his hand from hers as best she could.

Jernigan surged to his feet. "I'll tell you. Provided it's okay with Ms. Garrett, and Waverly cuts the chain."

Ward dropped her hand, but raised the chain linking them together. "She sticks with me until I know she's not my man. Woman."

Jernigan cleared his throat. "Hannah, you have to give me the okay on the explanation. HQ confirmed he's FBI, but with the channels we have to go through, we don't have his full story. Yet."

She flashed Ward a nasty glance. "No, I'm sure he's legit." Everything he did screamed agent. What was the point in delaying anyway? He'd learn it all eventually. At least this way she could control how he found out.

Jernigan and Ward stood in some kind of stare down. Waverly raised the cutters.

Her almost-lover held his stance wide. Every muscle on his body appeared braced and ready to spring, but she knew he held himself in cool control. How strange she could read him so easily. Knew that he could know her secret.

"It's okay. Tell him," she whispered.

Both men looked her way. Ward looked surprised. Jernigan nodded then gestured for them both to sit.

Ward leaned forward in his chair, his eyes focused. Hannah angled her body as far from him as she could. Waverly sat down beside her. The bolt cutters clanged as he placed them on the table.

"Are you familiar with a man named Kyle Barton?" Jernigan asked Ward.

Kyle. Barton. The words swirled around in her head. Not a name…just words. She grew dizzy with the effort to suppress the memories. *She must be strong.*

"No, I haven't… Hannah are you okay?"

She brushed the hair from her face, drawing Ward's hand up, as well. He reached for her chin and tenderly guided her face toward him. "Hannah?"

His tenderness was her undoing. Lie or not, tenderness had been so lacking in her life she responded. But only to a point. He could know the truth, but she didn't have to listen.

She stood, rubbing her temples to wipe out the pain she knew she could never erase. "I can't…I can't hear this."

Hannah pulled away only to be stopped by the chain. That damn chain. She gripped the metal around her wrist, tugging as she tried to pull her hand free. The skin under the clasp reddened. The small bones of her hand ached with the effort to force it off.

"Get this off me. Now."

Even to her own ears her voice sounded panicked, like a defenseless, trapped animal.

No. She would never be that again. She had made that vow in the bright flare of a gunshot blast four years ago.

Hannah took a calming breath. *Do it just like the counselors taught you.* She forced her fingers to still and faced her adversary with a determined stare.

She held the chain between them. "Take it off," she told him, her voice firm with resolve.

"How do I know you won't run off during our discussion?"

"The only reason your butt isn't walking back to town is out of professional courtesy. You'd do well to remember that," Jernigan warned.

Ward seemed unfazed by the marshal's threat.

Waverly stood.

Jernigan cut off Waverly's forward movement with a hand. "She won't leave. I give you my word as a U.S. Marshal."

She glanced at Ward. Now it was his time to weigh and assess Jernigan. He'd obviously dismissed Waverly as no match. The moments stretched taut until Ward gave Jernigan a tight nod.

Ward's green gaze searched her face then probed her eyes. "Tell me you won't try to escape," he said.

She tried to avert her eyes, but couldn't. A few hours ago, she'd connected with this man before her on an elemental level she'd never experienced before. It was the first time she remembered not feeling wary or on guard. Some small part of her yearned to experience that connection again.

"I won't."

"Use the cutters," he said, his voice grim. Maybe he wanted some of that connection back, too.

Jernigan cocked his head. "To the table. Sit."

A muscle in Ward's jaw bunched, but he nodded. The two of them sat in the vinyl chairs in silence opposite one another. She felt strangely bereft.

Someone had painted a yellow daisy on both sides of the clear acrylic napkin holder on the table. The tip of one white petal was chipped at the edge. She swallowed a lump in her throat. The cheap holder was a sad reminder of all the napkin holders she'd left behind.

What *was* the matter with her? The stupid holder didn't mean a thing. Just a silly little device to hold paper to wipe fingers. She didn't even need one. A drawer or a decorative basket would work just as well. But she'd bought plenty of just such holders in her relocations. Looked as if she'd be buying another shortly. Why was she getting melancholy over that?

Jernigan gestured to the men sitting around the table. "The three of us are going to have a short little talk. Afterward, I'm going to personally escort Cassidy to the car."

He focused his sharp-eyed attention on Ward. "Waverly will drop you off at Hannah's apartment to get your vehicle. Then he'll stop by the office and pick up handcuff keys for Hannah. Cassidy, you're on your own."

Waverly moved toward them and positioned the chain between the blades. The sound of metal crunching as the bolt cutters hit home sounded freedom. At least of some sort.

8

WARD WATCHED as Hannah walked out of the kitchen. She held her head in that proud, stiff manner he'd witnessed countless times in the offices of Protter and Lane. But now their time in the elevator felt like a distant memory.

He adjusted in his seat. Not too distant. The heavy heat forming between his legs reminded him he still wanted her.

The front door opened and closed, and the muscles of his gut tensed.

Jernigan cocked his head. "She's probably just getting her luggage. We've installed a perimeter security system. She's safe."

Now that Hannah and her distracting presence were gone, he was free to express just how angry he was. "Enough of these games, man. Tell me what you have."

Jernigan turned toward Waverly. "Why don't you unpack the rest of our gear?"

The young marshal looked as though he wanted to argue. But an order was an order. With a curt nod, he followed the path Hannah had made to the door. After Waverly shut the door, Jernigan turned his way.

"Kyle Barton?" he asked.

Ward shook his head. "Never heard of him."

Jernigan didn't say anything more and leaned back in his chair, propping up the front two legs again. "He's a member of the Miami crime circuit. A big player."

"Hannah was involved in organized crime?" It was hard to imagine his sexy little suspect involved in the kind of things the Miami group was infamous for.

"Barton hid behind legitimate businesses, but was basically nothing more than a slick and charming hood. Muscled contractors, extorted small businesses, but a devoted member of the Chamber of Commerce. I can say without hesitation she did not know the extent of his crimes. He was a charismatic leader. He demanded complete devotion from his troops. In all things. Including the girlfriends."

Ward cursed low in his throat.

Jernigan nodded. "When Hannah turned against him, he vowed to kill her."

Ward's hands tightened into fists. He thought of his mother, and of the unknown man who'd threatened and killed her. Hannah had nailed it in the elevator. He wanted to hunt down and imprison every man who preyed on innocent women—that's why he'd joined the FBI. He couldn't turn his anger on his mother's killer, the police had never found him. But they did know who pursued Hannah. Right now he could focus his anger on Kyle Barton. "Where is the son of a bitch?"

"In prison. Or was. He escaped. We don't know where he is."

Fear zapped through his body. Now he understood Hannah's need to hide.

He'd dealt with criminals before. Plenty of them. Some were sly, others overly friendly, most were just stupid. But none of them were like Hannah. Was she truly innocent?

He turned and leaned against the sink. "How did she get involved with you?"

"The FBI had a man on the inside. He brought her to us for protection," Jernigan told him.

Ward wasn't surprised. The FBI regularly tried to infiltrate the inner circles of many of the crime syndicates. Similar to his reasons for joining P&L's staff.

"What happened?"

"Hannah, uh…saw something she wasn't supposed to. She became expendable to Barton. She fled. Our operative on the inside caught her and brought her in. I've never seen anyone like her before. Terrified, yet full of fight."

Ward cursed again. He pivoted, bracing his hands on the sink.

"After debriefing, Hannah testified against Barton. Her information led to several more arrests. Hannah's testimony put him away."

"Until yesterday," Ward said between clenched teeth. From the first, he'd sensed a spirit of honor in Hannah, and known all along, deep in his gut, she wasn't the one stealing from Protter and Lane. What was it Brett had said? Proving her innocent?

Jernigan nodded. "Until yesterday. We told her sit tight. She's hidden well. New name, new identity, even a new look. I doubt he has any idea of where she is. No need to panic, and then the blackout happened."

Ward could fill in the blanks from there.

"Why'd you single Hannah out as your suspect?" Jernigan asked.

Because it was easier than facing the overwhelming desire I had for her. Ward lowered his eyes. "The crime I'm investigating is perpetrated through the computer system. I narrowed my search to the three people who had access to the mainframe. Something about Hannah's résumé didn't settle well. Now I know why."

"And that is?" Jernigan asked.

"It's too perfect. Like mine. Her cover's good. When I found her at her apartment, and saw her shredding files—"

"Standard procedure."

"Yeah, well, it's also standard procedure for a criminal."

"Do you have anything concrete on her? You know the rules, no crimes under the program or you're out."

Ward shook his head. "It was all circumstantial on my part."

"That's what I thought. Hannah is as honest as they come."

Ward turned and looked out the window. Her responses to him in the elevator had been real. His blood flowed southward as he replayed every sensuous moment they'd spent together.

Get a grip.

A movement outside the window released the hold Hannah's alluring memory held on him. He spotted the graceful outline of Hannah. For a moment, he watched, mesmerized by her fluid movements as she strolled between the trees. The wind ruffled her hair, tangling it as he had with his fingers hours earlier.

His jaw tightened with his barely held anger. Someone had tried to hurt her. Might still be trying to hurt her. And, despite his best intentions, he may have put her life into even more danger.

Jernigan's bootsteps on the linoleum kitchen floor tore his attention away from the vision outside the window.

"Cassidy, if you plan to stick around awhile, and I think that you are, we need to set some ground rules."

He jerked. It had been too long since responding to his real name. "Fair enough."

"We keep a marshal inside with her at all times. Another patrols the grounds. This is our assignment, not yours. We hold jurisdiction."

Ward turned toward the marshal, ready to argue. Somewhere in the last few minutes, he'd taken on the responsibility to protect Hannah. He *needed* to protect her.

"*We're* in the business of protection. Let us do our job, Special Agent."

Even though every instinct in his body screamed only he was up to the task of looking after Hannah, he gave the marshal a curt nod.

"You also have to secure permission from Hannah for you to stay."

Ah, now there was the catch. Biting back every inborn trait and playing second fiddle to a marshal would be a cinch compared to getting Hannah to agree to his presence.

Those were the rules. He'd have to abide by them if he wanted to remain. To be near Hannah. To protect her.

Jernigan nodded toward the window. "No time like the present."

THE LAZY CADENCE of the locusts filled the night air. Hannah always loved sleeping in the outdoors with the locusts lulling her to sleep. Camping under the stars with her foster family seemed so long ago. A lifetime ago. Three actually.

She would have liked to sleep with the windows open, the night breezes fanning her face and the sounds of nature connecting her to her past. A happier past. But the marshals would never have allowed that.

This old wooden boat dock she'd found looked a little rickety. She tested it a few times with a few solid whacks. The sound disturbed a few of the birds who flew away, but soon the locusts returned to their mating call.

The gentle lapping of the waves along the shore masked her footsteps on the old wooden planks. With the image of the dock slipping into the water under her weight, she slid to her knees with a slow carefulness. Barely a creak. The dock, surprisingly, was very sturdy. Perhaps the drug dealer Waverly had spoken of had given it this aged appearance so as not to draw attention. She slipped off her shoes and plunged her feet into the water. *Ahh. Heaven.*

Then she heard the sound of dead leaves crunching beneath the soles of his running shoes. Ward.

No! She didn't want him here. He was a liar and a

user. She pulled her feet from the water and hugged her knees to her chest.

But what was she? She'd lied to him.

Hannah turned her head sending him a glare.

The moon had risen high in the dark night sky. Why'd it have to be so bright? Couldn't she have caught a break and gotten a moonless night so she didn't have to see his rugged handsomeness? Or feel the deep longing in her heart.

She could tell by the softness of his expression Jernigan had told him everything. But the muscles around his lips were drawn tight. He was angry. Well, he wasn't the first person to blame her for her predicament. Blame her for her weakness.

She turned around and thrust her feet back into the water. But the gently swaying coolness didn't give her the same kind of relaxation it had just moments before. Why'd he have to come out here anyway?

The wood creaked as he dropped beside her. She watched as he removed his shoes and socks. Droplets of water sprayed her legs as he plunged his feet into the water beside her.

"I see why you're out here. This feels great."

Hannah's stomach knotted at his nearness. The memory of his lips and his betrayal singed her every nerve ending. Then a breeze blew from off the water and cooled her rising temper. She could be just as nonchalant.

The wind blew a lock of hair into her eyes. The remaining links of chain clanked against the metal around her wrist as she brushed the hair from her face.

Ward exhaled roughly. "Here, give me your hand and I'll take care of that."

She looked at him for the first time since he sat beside her. "I thought you didn't have a key."

"I don't. Just give me your hand. Please."

She'd much rather suffer with the handcuff around her wrist than have him help her. Or touch any part of her body. But when he said *please,* his voice open, maybe for the first time, it drew her into his spell. Like the force he'd had her under in the elevator before she'd come to her senses.

With a jerky, reluctant movement, she held out her arm.

His long, warm fingers wrapped around her forearm, sending a shaft of sensation up to her elbow and down to her fingers. She gasped as fingers of his other hand grazed the chafed skin under the handcuff.

He looked up, the greenness of his eyes dark in the moonlight. "Sorry about that. I'll try to be gentle."

Why'd that have to remind her of his gentle caresses in the elevator?

"Now hold your hand flat."

Before she could respond, Ward reached into his pocket and pulled out a tool with a long, thin top. He fit the tip into the lock and began to turn it with slow precise movements.

He was picking the lock.

"This doesn't seem like something an agent with the FBI should be able to do."

He gave her a mischievous smile. "I have many hidden talents."

Like demonstrating with his lips the true meaning of toe-curling. Like his caresses that were tender and caused her skin to heat at the same time. Like what he did with his tongue…

She sucked in a breath, and he looked up.

"Stop being distracting. Just a few more…there."

The lock clicked and the cuff sprang open, sending blessed relief to her wrist. "That's how you were able to get into my apartment. You picked the lock." She rubbed at the reddened skin.

"I did knock. You probably didn't hear me over the shredding." He tossed the cuff aside, banging it on the wooden plank. "Here, let me look at it."

She didn't want him touching her, but he already had her wrist turned up for his inspection before she could protest.

He moved her arm left and right, allowing the moonlight to illuminate her skin. Ward leaned forward placing a tiny kiss on the delicate skin. "I'm sorry."

Shuddering sensations emanated from where his lips touched. Her mouth went dry and without effort she leaned toward him.

Then, as if a bolt of lightning were racing up her spine, she pulled her hand from his. "You thought I was some kind of criminal," she accused.

Damn, she hated the shrill tone her voice had taken on. It showed that she cared. That it hurt.

Ward picked up one of the stones lying on the dock. With a flick of his wrist, he tossed it across the water. The stone skipped twice then sank. "I didn't want you to be."

"Oh? What's that supposed to mean?" But she couldn't

help but smile. His voice sounded almost boyish, like someone trying to still convince themselves of Santa.

Another stone. This one managed to skip three times. "I had a plan."

"Oh, really? Were you planning on asking for a date in, say, ten to twenty?"

His next stone only went one bounce. "No, I was going to hire you the best lawyer I could find. Maybe swing an immunity deal."

Hannah slumped beside him, her earlier bravado spent. In some weird kind of federal agent way, his plan was kind of sweet. He'd thought her some kind of computer outlaw. As an officer of the law, more than likely, he held any type of thief in the highest contempt. Oh, he'd bring her to justice, but he'd find some way to protect her at the same time.

Her earlier outrage faded. No one had ever tried to shield her before. Kyle hadn't. The marshals had offered protection because it was their job. Ward had wanted to defend her.

He raised his arm to fling another stone.

"Here, let me show you how it's done." She ignored the fissure of spark as her fingers brushed his. With a deft flick of the wrist, she tossed the stone.

Ward whistled beside her. "Six skips. That's pretty impressive."

"That's nothing. I've gone as high as eight."

The beam of car headlights drew their attention.

"That's my ride back to town," Ward told her.

"Oh." Hannah couldn't understand the flood of sad anger that washed over her.

She reached for another rock, but his warm hand stilled hers. "Look, Hannah. I want you to know that I see you as more than just…"

"Than your usual tumble in an elevator," she finished for him.

He chuckled softly. A sound she vowed to memorize. The memory would keep her warm long after the summer sun faded and the long cold nights of winter took over. "Not someone I'm likely to forget."

He stood and Hannah followed him. Reluctant to face him, she knew the moment for goodbye had come. She'd said a thousand goodbyes over her lifetime. But this time was different. This time she'd allowed someone to get close.

Jernigan had warned her from the start to avoid entanglements. She knew the reason behind his caution. Now she felt the repercussions.

The lights of the sedan beamed again. Ward brushed the hair from her face. Her heart constricted at the strange pain of this goodbye. She closed her eyelids so as not to look at him. She knew the darkness would not be able to mask the emotions in her eyes.

"I'd like to stay."

Those four words echoed around her. This time their gazes locked.

"I know I'm the last person you want hanging around," he said.

She lost her train of thought as he tucked her hair behind her ear. He was saying something about leaving because she wanted him to go.

She shook her head. "No, it's not that."

"I know what happened in the elevator was an aberration. I won't expect anything like that."

But would she?

"There's a spare bedroom in the safe house. I can commute to the city for the few days you're here. Think of me as another guard," he told her.

Yes, think of him as that. Only as a guard. Not as a potential lover.

Moments ago her soul had ached at the thought of saying goodbye to this man. It looked like fate might be giving her just a little longer to be with him. Dare she take it?

Another breeze blew off the lake and she shivered. Ward drew her closer to him. His hand drifted from behind her ear to trace the outline of her cheek and down her jaw to rest on her chin. The rough pad of his thumb rested just below the softness of her lips.

"Yes, I'd like you to stay."

Her heart raced as he lowered his head.

The beep of his watch broke their near contact. His hands fell away. Ward pressed a button on the face. "It's midnight. End to the longest day of the year."

"Yes, the days will only get shorter."

He dropped his hand and they took a few steps away from each other.

Ward nodded his head toward the car. "Waverly's going to take me back to town so I can pick up a few things and follow him in my car. After that, there will always be two people with you."

He reached for her hand and gave it a little squeeze. "Try to get some sleep."

Ward turned and walked toward the car. The sad song of the locusts filled the air, only to be broken by the revving of the engine.

Hannah watched as the taillights of the sedan faded into the trees. Once more she was alone. She took a deep breath, filling her lungs full of the cleansing air of the country.

She'd survived another compromising situation.

9

THE BRISK SPRAY of the shower made Hannah feel almost human again. As she soaped her arms and legs, memories of Ward's lips running across her skin made her knees go weak. The soft skin of her breasts showed a red, slightly roughened place where his Saturday no-shave stubble had deliciously scratched her.

She wondered what his fellow suits at the Bureau would think of his lax use of a razor? Tough guys or not, FBI agents always struck her as a bunch of squares. Except for one. She allowed her mind to drift to the other FBI agent in her life. Jim. The man who'd saved her life, and died while doing it.

Her throat constricted and tears came to her eyes, but she blinked them back. Tears were in her past. She'd left them behind when she left her old identity. Only the guilt remained.

She scrubbed herself briskly with the washcloth as if the action could wipe away any remaining trace of Ward Colem— Cassidy. Drying off quickly, she stepped onto the towel acting as a bath mat. The marshals were good, but they didn't secure much in the way of creature comforts.

Shivering slightly, Hannah reached for the plastic sack containing her clothes. After stepping into a pair of white cotton panties, she cinched her terry cloth, no-nonsense robe around her middle.

The cramped little bathroom had also missed the former owner's decorating touch. The fading flowers of the wallpaper yielded to cabinets that she suspected had, at one time, been painted cream. Now the yellowed paint flaked off to reveal a beautiful dark wood. Who would paint over something that could be restored with a little elbow grease? What other secrets did this house hold?

She tugged opened a cabinet and stuffed her toiletries inside. Hannah was too tired to do her normal nightly moisturizing routine. All she needed tonight was a comb.

Steam from her shower fogged the mirror. Hannah pulled the towel from her head to wipe the moisture away. The harshness of the bathroom light revealed a face red from scrubbing with the washcloth. She searched for a way to lessen the light's effect, but the fixture covering the bulb had cracked and broken off casting an uneven light over the room. She'd just have to live with it tonight, but that would be something the marshals would have to fix tomorrow.

With slow swipes of the comb, she removed a few tangles at the ends. Hannah kind of liked the red highlights in her hair. She'd never been red before. It sort of gave her a feisty air. She liked that. What would her new hair color be? If she ever stayed in one place long enough to invest some money, a hair rinse company would be her first choice. She alone sank enough money to keep the business afloat.

Tangles gone, she gave her head a shake to fluff her hair. She'd let it dry naturally. Slipping into her house shoes, she opened the bathroom door and stuck her head outside. The lake house appeared to be empty. Waverly and Ward would not have had time yet to return from the city. The trip here took at least forty-five minutes. Jernigan had said something about checking the perimeter and was apparently outside.

More than likely, this would be her last time alone until the marshals dropped her into her new assignment. Her new identity.

Don't get melancholy.

Right, this was just the way things were. Every person had their burden. Hers just happened to be starting a completely new life every few years. Some people might even think of it as an adventure. A way to wipe away all the past mistakes and start again.

What she needed was a cup of hot herbal tea. Before her last foster mother had died, she'd always brewed a pot whenever things looked grim. It was one of the few good memories Hannah held dear. She walked into the kitchen, the shock of the quaint room, after passing through the living room, still had not dulled.

A cardboard box rested on one of the cabinets, filled with cooking utensils. After the fuss she'd made last time when no teakettle had been provided, she knew Waverly would make sure that item was included. Waverly had been brought on last time after Jernigan's original partner retired.

She liked Waverly. He had a nice smile. If things were different, and she was like any normal kind of girl, she could have been with someone uncomplicated like him.

But he didn't give her the sense of security Ward did. Nor the element of danger. And she was a gal who craved a little danger in a man. Excellent, her poor taste in men hadn't altered.

Even with her wet hair, sweat broke out on the back of her neck. Her nipples tightened as she imagined all the dangerous things Ward could do to her body. And her heart.

Get your mind off him.

Well, that was going to be hard to do seeing as how she'd practically invited him to stay with her. The harsh criticism of Kyle Barton blasted in her mind, bright and accusatory. She *was* a stupid bitch.

Hannah liked all but the stupid part. She'd changed since the last time she'd seen Kyle. Now she'd like to show him the true meaning behind bitch.

Her thoughts drifted to Ward and she immediately saw the contrast. Both men might hold an air of danger, but Kyle's was vindictive and cruel. While Ward…a shiver raced down her spine.

They would just have to set up a few ground rules. That was all. No personal conversation. No being alone together. No kissing. No thoughts of sex. No thoughts.

What was she thinking inviting him here? Maybe she should acknowledge that stupid descriptor after all. With a disgusted sigh, Hannah turned her attention to her search for the teakettle. After rummaging through the box, she found the kettle and a popular women's magazine. She knew this was Waverly's doing. With a smile, she placed the magazine on the table. A hot mug of tea and taking a quiz on her personal sense of style. What could be better?

Hannah poured water into the kettle. Oh, she could have just heated up a coffee cup of water in the microwave, but it somehow didn't hold the same appeal. The act of putting the kettle on the stove filled her with a sense of familiarity. She'd seen her foster mother do it a hundred times. Funny, she'd been thinking about her a lot lately.

With a deft flick of her wrist, she turned the stove knob to high and settled down with her magazine. She'd brew her tea and think things through later. An article on the cover about decorating with scarves caught her attention.

The kettle began to whistle, and she slid her feet into her slippers. She poured the steaming liquid into her mug and inhaled the revitalizing mint aroma. She'd just resettled herself when headlights flashed through the window then cut off.

She caught her breath with a mixture of hope and dread. She didn't need to make a guess to figure out who it was. Ward. Ward was home.

No. Do not think of this place as home.

She could ignore him. Maybe he wouldn't come in. Who was she kidding? He was here to protect her. And after their heated exchanges in the elevator, she knew he wouldn't avoid her. Ward possessed a steely determination—most of the agents she'd known did, and there'd be no skirting around the issue. The sex issue.

She yearned for his lips, his large hands, his…damn.

Even the briefest thought of sex with Ward filled her with burning need.

Ground rules. They needed to get those set right away. Besides, she didn't run from confrontation. The last time she'd run was four years ago, and she'd regretted it ever since.

Hannah yanked the belt around her robe tighter and walked toward the front room in slow, deliberate steps. Okay, she'd face him, but she didn't have to do it quickly.

The three men were just closing the front door behind them when Hannah entered the black-and-white room. She avoided looking at the sensual portrait on the wall.

Waverly and Ward chuckled over something. Guess the mini testosterone feud brewing between those two had vanished. But Ward's laugh, the deep rich tones coming from his chest, somehow reminded her of the groans he'd made when they were kissing.

Screw the ground rules. Hannah's gaze didn't just drift to Ward, it zoomed. As if sensing her attention, his face lost its humorous expression and their gazes met. His green eyes darkened. A pulse at his temple beat rapidly.

The tempo of her own heartbeat quickened and her lips parted. His gaze dropped to her mouth.

Waverly lugged something behind him and placed it on one of the black lacquered tables. "Ward brought the TV from his apartment. The replay of the evening news should be starting soon and we can check your cover."

Hannah broke her contact with Ward and looked toward Jernigan.

"You may be able to stay in your current placement if your cover's not blown," he told her, his tone neutral.

She released her breath on a happy sigh. "It never occurred to me that I could stay—"

Jernigan raised a cautionary finger. "*May*, Hannah. Don't get your hopes up."

"We stopped at a convenience store on the way out of town, but the late edition of the newspaper wasn't out yet," Ward told her.

She nodded, not trusting herself to speak. Maybe, just maybe she'd be able to keep her hair, her black walls, her yellow stars, her name. It was the first time she'd ever made up a name on her own.

Waverly stood and turned on the TV with the remote. Snowy white fuzz from the screen filled the room. Hannah automatically walked to the wall and flipped the light off. Waverly changed channels, but the snow never changed. "Your TV is crap, Cassidy."

"There's nothing wrong with the TV, just the way you set it up." Ward walked forward and took the remote from Waverly's hand.

"We'll never pick up anything like this, I'll order a satellite dish tomorrow." Jernigan said in an "I'll solve this" tone of voice.

Great, more testosterone.

"Did anyone try the antenna?" she asked.

Three sets of male eyes glanced her way. Hannah looked from one tough guy law enforcement officer to another. "You are all pathetic. Did everyone in the room grow up with cable?"

"Hannah…" Waverly began talking in that appeasing tone men used when they thought they knew more than a woman.

Hannah marched to the closet, and pulled it open. She grabbed a bent wire hanger suspended from a piece of rope where a wooden rod must have been. With each step toward the TV, she untwisted the metal hanger. With a few adjustments, she fitted the end into the slot where the antenna would have been.

White snow still filled the screen, and she almost felt the wave of male satisfaction wash over her. Then she moved up the dial. Channel five came in, fuzzy, but with perfect sound and in color.

"Remind me never to ask any of you to check my car," she told them as she sat down on the couch.

The opening song of the evening news sounded. The camera zoomed in on a blond wearing a serious face, but a smile in her voice. "The recent controlled power outage of the downtown area caught two city workers unaware in an elevator."

The screen cut to one of the firefighters who'd taken her vitals. "Although they'd only been trapped a few hours, the temperatures inside the cage were in the high nineties and rising. With no water, they would have been facing severe dehydration and heat stroke in no time."

She knew their situation had been getting worse, but not to those kind of proportions. Hannah shuddered.

Ward took a few steps toward her and placed his arm on her shoulder. Startled, she looked up at him, but his interest remained on the TV screen. He probably hadn't realized he'd made the comforting gesture. But it was comforting, oh, yes it was. The warmth from his palm seeped into her shoulder and radiated throughout her entire body.

Just breathe in and out. Now if only she could make her heart take up a more normal beat.

She looked back at the TV. The next shot was of Ward. Although it was shot through the glass, the hard planes of his jawline and his lips curving into a soft smile just for her were clearly visible. She sucked in her breath as she realized he was looking down at her now. Although the camera had only managed to get the back of her red hair.

She remembered that moment. He'd been offering to drive her home. They hadn't even known a cameraman was around at that point. The reporter talked, but Hannah's sole focus was only on the scene playing before her.

Her image was walking toward the door now. *This was it.* Her face blurred then an arm, Ward's arm, blocked her from view of the lens.

The hand on her shoulder gave a little squeeze, and she exhaled the breath she hadn't realized she'd been holding. He'd protected her then. He was protecting her now. If she weren't careful, she could fool herself into thinking it was more.

She stood, his hand falling off her shoulder. She walked to the remote and turned the TV on mute as the anchor smiled her way into the next story.

Jernigan leaned back against the cushions of the couch. "Hmm," was all he said.

A bubble of hope rose to the back of her throat. She

swallowed hard before that longing lodged permanently.

"I think we can work with this. What did they get? A good shot of your hair, and blurred image of your face. Not recognizable." Jernigan stood and began to pace. "You've been in Gallem shy of a year. In all that time…nothing from our informant network. We haven't gotten so much as a blip in any of our intelligence."

Ward snorted. "Marshal intelligence. Isn't that an oxymoron?"

Jernigan raised an eyebrow. "We took you down, didn't we?"

Ward nodded his agreement. "It took two of you."

Hannah looked from Fed to Marshal. Their words were serious, but their stances didn't look combative. But rather some weird, male-bonding positions.

"Cassidy, why don't you show us what you can do to get the story of your little lockup in the elevator off the front page?" Jernigan suggested.

Ward drummed his fingers along the back of the couch, close to the exposed skin of her neck. "Done."

Some sort of plan was in the works, but they'd neglected to let her in on the deal. "Can someone tell me what's going on here?"

Jernigan stopped his pacing and turned to look at her. "Hannah, you have some time off coming your way?"

"Yes, I uh, I haven't taken any leave."

"Perfect. That should give us enough time to see if anyone from Miami makes their move. Hannah, in the morning, call your boss and tell him you're sick. You don't know how long you'll be out, but you'll be in touch."

"Okay."

"Ward, you keep an eye on Hannah's desk. See if she gets any visitors at work, any strange mail. I'll have someone check her apartment and tap her phone."

"Wouldn't he just grab her?" Ward asked.

"No, that's not Barton's MO. He plays with minds. He likes cat and mouse."

Humiliation and fear, she added silently.

Hannah turned from the three men, hugging her arms about her waist. She knew his games all too well. "Last time he began with notes. First at work, then home. Cut out pictures of eyes. We're watching you." Her last words came out on a whisper.

"We pulled her right away."

She stood and walked toward a small, bricked-up fireplace, away from Ward. Away from all the horrible memories he dredged up. Hannah closed her eyes as if trying to block out Kyle's ability to find her, see her anywhere. "The time before there were calls, but those started at home first."

Hannah sensed Ward's nearness before she felt his hands on her shoulders. She wanted to take a step back. To lean into him and feel his broad chest against her shoulders. To have his warm arms hold her close.

Taking a step away, she forced her arms out of the protective gesture and down to her sides.

"I'm going to organize the diversion," Ward said.

She turned and watched as Ward pulled his cell phone out of his pocket and opened the front door, slamming it behind him. She didn't want to be anywhere near the front door when he came back. "I'm going to finish my tea in the kitchen. I didn't pack an alarm clock, so someone will need to wake me so I can call Mr. Protter."

"No problem."

Hannah turned toward the kitchen and poured herself another cup of tea. The water had cooled, but was still warm enough to soothe. Wrapping her fingers around the mug, she walked to the window. It was too dark to make anything out, but she pictured the dock where she and Ward had skipped stones.

She'd irritated Ward when she moved away. Why had he asked to stay? Why had she agreed? Somewhere, deep in her soul, she knew if she'd told Ward she didn't want him there, he wouldn't have come back.

It was his honor. She'd encountered that strict responsibility all those years ago when she'd made her escape from Kyle and his thugs. Jim. Hannah hadn't allowed herself to think of him since he'd died. She squeezed her eyes tight to prevent the image of him coming into sight. The guilt. But it was too late. The tough FBI agent who'd infiltrated Kyle's group in Miami had saved her life.

When she'd asked him why, he'd replied without hesitation that it was his duty. To his country and to innocent people like her.

Hannah understood that same sense of duty lay in Ward's heart, too. Not to the cause, but to her. He felt a responsibility to her. Because they'd been so intimate. Sexual attraction. Biological reaction. *Reduce it to nothing.*

Hot, curl-her-toes, make-her-think-of-nothing-else

kind of sexual desire. Her nipples tightened and the
flesh between her legs tingling thinking of his warm, soft
lips kissing her neck, licking her ear, tracing the curve
of her bra with his tongue.

Stop it.

She whirled from the window, sloshing the liquid on
her hand and down her sleeve.

"Damn."

Placing the now-empty mug onto the countertop,
she flung her wet hand over the sink. She reached for
the tap and rinsed her hand.

They'd taught her better than to act like that. Jim's
memory deserved more.

Ward would have to go.

The emergency workers had halted their activities in
the elevator. But what about the next time? And the
next? She'd lost her identity enough times to know it
was a painful, frustrating process. Having him around
would make it worse. Yes, he'd have to go.

She would absolve him of his duty. *Hey, it was a fun
almost-roll-in-the-hay, but now it's time for you to go.*
Heck, by now, he was probably already regretting his
gallant urge to come back. He'd probably latch on to
any excuse to escape.

The front door opened and closed. Ward had
returned. She would tell him he could go now. After
washing out her teacup, she placed it on the dish rack
to dry. Cinching her robe tighter, she headed back into
the front room to tell Ward.

Ward wasn't there. Only Waverly. Lamplight glinted
off the barrel of his gun as he checked for bullets. He

slipped the gun in his belt. She also noticed his cuff case. She assumed he'd picked up his keys while at the office. "Sorry. I'm about to start my night watch."

"It's okay." She'd been around guns enough not to let them startle her. First with Kyle and his "associates" and then again with all the law enforcement. She even had her own gun in her bedside table at home. Damn. It was still there. New town, new protection. She did have her Taser.

Should she ask Waverly where she could locate Ward? No. The marshals probably already guessed there was something going on between them. She didn't want them to know about her involvement with the agent. Potential involvement.

With a wave, she turned and headed for the narrow hallway leading to her room. Hannah had just reached the bathroom when the door opened. Ward emerged wearing nothing but his boxer shorts.

She swallowed. Hard.

Yes, it was just as she suspected. He was gorgeous nearly naked. All that skin of his she'd felt, tasted... lightly tanned from the sun, stretched taut over hard-won muscles. A pioneer woman could wash shirts on his stomach. A light dusting of hair sealed the perfect package. She hadn't gotten a good glance at him outside the elevator. Barefoot and shirtless, he looked like some Greek god. Achilles, the man of strength...but even he had one glitch in the armor.

"Hi," she managed to mumble. She sounded like an idiot.

"The marshals put me in the room next to yours." His

voice sounded normal, professional, but heat and hunger burned in the green depths of his eyes.

"I'll be sleeping on your schedule, so I won't be taking any night shifts until the weekend. But I'm a light sleeper and should hear if anything unusual goes on in your room."

Was that supposed to be reassuring? It sounded more like a promise. She nodded, trying to make her tone match his. "Yes, uh, that makes sense. Thank you."

He took another step out of the bathroom. Light from the fixture poured through the darkened hallway. She shrank back into the shadows.

"Are you okay?" he asked.

"Would you turn off the bathroom light? It's a little too bright for this late at night."

Ward smiled, and reached behind him for the switch. "Sure, no problem."

The hallway plummeted into darkness except for the traces of light from the front room. But she could still make out every outline of Ward's handsome, blond body.

She took a step around him so she could make it to her room, but he caught her wrist. Her skin underneath his fingertips heated. "Hannah, look at me," he urged, his voice sweet temptation.

Taking a breath, she lifted her gaze. What could it hurt to look at him? It was dark, good cover.

"I know you're avoiding me, and I think I know why."

"You do?"

"Yes, it's because of what happened between us in the elevator."

She averted her eyes.

"You're uncomfortable with it, I know. But look, despite the fact that I'm not a marshal officially assigned to watch over you, I know the boundaries."

Hannah met his stare again. "And those are?"

His eyes lowered to her lips. "No kissing. You'll have to stay at arm's length."

Surprise forced her to swallow. Was he actually suggesting that she wanted *him* to kiss *her?* That he was denying her? That he had to hold her back? That jerk.

Hannah opened her mouth to tell him off. Those weren't just her moans in the elevator. Elemental protests from her old self surged forward. With a barely imperceptible movement, the robe slipped off her shoulder. His gaze darted to her bared skin.

She'd show him wanting. She stepped closer. "Oh, really now," she said. Her voice pure innocence. And challenge.

She wasn't about to let him get away with denying his desire. Okay, a complete one-eighty from her earlier decision of telling him to leave, but then he was the one who basically offered up the dare.

Ward cleared his throat. "Yes."

She gave him a slight smile, and moved even nearer. The scent from his aftershave filled her nose. She stood close enough to know the crisp hairs on his chest were a darker blond than those on his head. "There's one thing we didn't do in the elevator," she told him as she moved her hand toward his body.

He opened his mouth as if to speak, but her finger tracing the outline of his nipple stopped his words. He engulfed her smaller hand in his, preventing further movement.

She licked her lips. His gaze shot back to her mouth. It was the game she'd played in his office just yesterday morning. "We didn't have a goodbye kiss."

"Oh, well—"

Her lips on his stopped the rest of his sentence. For a moment, his lips stretched straight, probably in shock. Then they softened, not returning the kiss, but definitely not rebuffing it, either.

Then with a groan, his arms circled around her waist, drawing her to him. He opened his lips, darting his tongue into her mouth.

This is a game. But a flood of wanting washed throughout her body, pooling between her legs. One of his hands moved to her hair. He sank his fingers into the wet loose strands, cradling her head.

Urgent desire zinged from every pore of her body. Her breasts hurt with the need to feel his lips. He drew away, his hands dropping to her hips, pushing her back. Her body silently cried out with thwarted longing.

They stood in the darkness touching only with the gentlest of kisses. She longed for the sweet tenderness of his lips to go on forever.

But it had to stop.

He pulled away completely. The cool rush of air between them an unwelcome relief from the heat. The light streaming from under his bedroom door was a painful reminder that they not only came from two different worlds, but would soon leave for two different places.

"Goodbye, Ward."

He stepped aside and let her pass, but he didn't move toward his own room. She realized he was waiting to see her safely inside her room. Like a good protector. Like a good officer of the law taking care of his responsibility.

As she shut the door behind her, she heard Ward say goodbye. His bare feet near silent as he padded to his own room.

Her room remained dark except for the ambient light from the window. Jernigan would probably yell at her for keeping the drapes open, but she liked nature. Had missed it while living in Gallem. Waverly stood watch right now anyway. He wouldn't hassle her over the silly curtain.

Unlooping the belt, Hannah shrugged out of the robe and placed it on the edge of the bed. She settled under the cool sheets, pulling the covers to her nose.

But nothing could cloak the raw tingling of her lips. She'd made a mistake. *Huge.* Where had this stupid temper of hers come from? She'd never been one to challenge or provoke. But from the beginning, Ward had drawn something from her.

She heard the click of his bedside lamp turning off through the thinness of the walls. The springs creaked as he shifted in the bed. Did he sleep in the boxers or out?

She rolled onto her side, hitting her pillow a few times in frustration.

An ache settled into her heart, and she pinched her arm so she wouldn't feel sorry for herself. An old habit. She hadn't pinched herself since her foster mother died and she ended up in the group home.

Tomorrow she'd tell him he didn't need to stay.

Tomorrow.

Tonight she would sleep knowing his head rested next to hers, his body lay sprawled beside her, separated only by the wall.

10

HE WAS IN HELL.

His nerve endings were wound so tight, it wouldn't be long before he snapped like a rubber band.

The thin walls separating their beds didn't mask the little sounds she made as she slept. Little sighs that reminded him of her moans as he'd plunged his tongue into her mouth. Like the tuner on a radio, his body aligned to her pitch and frequency.

Around three in the morning he debated about pushing the bed to the other side of the room. As his bare feet touched the cold linoleum, he heard, *actually heard* the sheet against her skin as she turned in her sleep.

Squeezing his eyes shut, he rolled back onto the bed, covering his head with the pillow.

Sometime in the wee hours of the morning, his body finally allowed him to doze in some exhausted sleep. But images of Hannah haunted him even there. He almost didn't hear the alarm. The bright sunlight streamed through the open curtains. Rubbing his eyes, he made his way to the hall. And nearly dropped his black toiletry bag when Hannah stepped out of the bathroom.

She greeted him in little more than a towel. The blue terry cloth was more enticing than the voluminous folds of her robe. His blood pressure soared as the towel slipped lower, revealing more and more of the swell of her breasts.

He very nearly groaned.

"Morning, Ward."

"Humph."

She pulled the towel higher, making her cleavage more pronounced. "Would you like me to pour you some orange juice while you're in the shower?"

Only if she poured it in his lap. "Uh, no. I want to get to work early."

Hannah grabbed the ends of the towel with one hand and pushed the tangled length of her hair away from her eyes. "I think the only relief from this heat would be to run around naked."

His toiletry bag banged to the floor.

"Here, let me get that for you." As she bent below him, he could have had a clear view down to her navel. If he were jerk enough to take a peek. His eyes nearly popped out of his head.

She handed the bag to him, her fingers brushing in too long a contact against his arm.

"Eric watched the morning news and said there was nothing about us at all."

"Who's Eric?"

"Waverly. You know, your fellow officer."

What was she doing calling him Eric? What was he doing getting on a first-name basis with her? Nothing ticked him off more than…

Than what? For another man to talk to her? Look at her? Desire her? Kiss her?

All the things he'd done and more. Still wanted to do.

Was he getting territorial? *You're losing it, buddy.*

No, that was the problem—he wasn't losing it. The minute he got anywhere near her, all the blood left his brain and went straight to his—

"I left the newspaper for you on the kitchen table. It's amazing how successful Gallem law enforcement was in the wee hours this morning. Not only did they nab several key players in an art scam, they managed to locate stolen vehicles worth millions."

He lifted an eyebrow. "Oh yeah? Good for them."

"All that crime fighting had the added bonus of relegating a little story of two people trapped in an elevator to page thirty-two."

"And all thanks to the men and women in blue."

Her smile deepened. Her towel gaped in the front, flashing him a lot of the skin he'd touched plenty in the elevator, but never had the chance to see.

She gave him a playful slap on the arm. "Stop being so coy. You created quite a diversion."

So did she.

"I'm impressed."

So was he.

"I made some coffee for you."

Why was he standing here talking to her?

The rich aroma of coffee wafted through the air. He hated the stuff, but maybe he should give the bitter drink another shot if the sight of Hannah would jump-start his mornings like this.

He pivoted, ready to tell her he didn't want any stinking coffee, but the concern on her face stopped any harsh words. Yeah, pathetic jerk, taking his frustrations out on her.

"Not much of a coffee drinker. But thanks."

Her eyebrows puckered, creating a delicate little line he wanted to kiss. "But you're always drinking it with Protter."

Ward chuckled. "That's undercover work."

The cute little line disappeared. Her face clearly showed skepticism now. "Uh-huh."

"Law enforcement in action."

Hannah laughed, an erotic throaty sound. Her laugh quickened the blood in his veins.

He shouldn't have kissed her last night. He knew what she was about, trying to make him admit he wanted her. His instincts told him to back away. Far away. But when she'd touched his chest and kissed him, he hadn't been able to resist.

Her laugh died, but she was still smiling. A smile for him.

He pushed around her into the bathroom. The sooner he got out of there and got their relationship on an impersonal footing, the better off they both would be. Anything other than detached professionalism would hinder his performance both as a protector and as an agent.

"Is everything okay, Ward?"

She was the very picture of innocent female obliviousness. Good. He was behaving like an idiot.

"I'm fine. Just missing my morning juice jolt. Do you want anything while I'm out?"

Her mouth closed, and she blinked a few times. After a moment, she shook her head. "No. Uh, thank you."

With a nod, he closed the bathroom door, and took a deep breath.

The air still held the herbal scent of her shampoo, and his body hardened even more. He turned on the water spigot.

He was trying to do the right thing here. Hannah had to keep her towels, ice and sleeping sighs away from him. For good measure, she had to stop smiling, bending and generally being in his vicinity.

Especially in the morning, when he'd just woken up hard from dreams filled with her. Hannah's timing this morning had been so perfect, he would almost suspect she'd planned the thing.

Except she looked so damned innocent, and he'd accused her once of deceit. To his regret. He wasn't about to do it again.

Despite the tedious paper trails he'd have to track, today he actually looked forward to work. He'd much rather spend the day drinking coffee and acting the tough guy with Protter than being the nice guy with Hannah. Hell, it would be a relief to face an ordinary criminal rather than Hannah's erotic assault. Maybe he could arrest somebody. Maybe they'd resist apprehension, and he'd get to chase them. Perfect.

A knock sounded at the bathroom door.

"Ward, I thought of something we need. Ice."

He twisted the faucet all the way to cold. He'd need it.

Damn, damn, damn.

He was thoughtful.

Of course, she should have known that already. He'd been an unselfish lover in the elevator. Her skin tingled as her body remembered just how unselfish he'd been. She had been the selfish one.

She was just about to tell him it would be better if he left. That they should never see each other again. And then he had to go and be thoughtful, asking her if she wanted anything when he went to the store.

Damn him.

All her thoughts shifted to wanting him to stay. And, oh, how she wanted him to remain in this cabin with her by the lake. But it was dangerous. The mandatory therapy with a shrink prepared her for possibly forming attachments to the various marshals who'd protected her over time. But no relationships had come.

Her first marshal had been too old, more like the kindly, protective father she'd longed for. Jernigan was too prickly and by-the-book. Two safe houses with him, and she still didn't know his first name. Waverly was someone she liked to spend time with, but he was more like a puppy than a lover. A puppy with a gun, but still not someone she could form any kind of link with.

But with Ward, it was all different. She'd been pulled to him long before he protected her. She sensed his strength. Sensed his security. Sensed his danger.

He wanted her, but fought the pull between them. Why she didn't know. Although it was probably some sort of noble male idea of saving her from something. He possessed a deep-rooted honor.

And suddenly her decision was made. This was not a battle she intended to let him win. In all these years, she'd never had these kinds of desires. Urges to know a man for more than what she needed from him in or out of bed.

Ward was seduction itself. A heady mix of danger and tenderness. This was her one shot. Her one chance to feel real passion before having to leave him forever.

WARD STAYED in Gallem as long as he could. He dropped by the office, but with the electricity still being diverted to the suburbs, the downtown work area resembled a ghost town. Driving around the building, he looked for anything suspicious. Finding nothing, he headed back to his own apartment.

He managed to spend the next few hours reworking his case, and not thinking of Hannah. Some of the documentation he'd requested from Washington had arrived, and he pored over it. He still waited for information from the island bank someone from P&L was using to stash their cash. Not an easy task, but sometimes they would cooperate.

He was closer. Someone had done a good job of planting quite a few red herrings. All pointing toward Hannah. She would have made a convenient scapegoat. Fortunately for her, she had friends in high places. That's why it was important for him to be so thorough with his paper tracking, to protect the innocent as much as to unveil the bad guy. He leaned back in his chair.

"What do you know? Guess James did teach me something." Not that he'd ever tell her.

It would probably take him a week to wrap things

up. He could probably angle for another using the excuse of paperwork. Either way, he wouldn't be needed after that. Either Hannah was compromised and on her way to her new identity. Or she stayed and he went back to D.C. Two weeks. Two weeks max.

As the sun began to set, he powered down his laptop and locked up. On his way out of town, he stopped by the grocery store.

Afterward, an impulse made him take the turn to Hannah's apartment rather than merging onto the highway and heading for the safe house. Parking a block away from her complex, he took a meandering path to her apartment. He walked casually by her door, giving the knob the briefest of glances as he passed. He spotted no signs of forced entry or tampering.

Relief worked its way through his body. Strange. He'd suffered through surveillance before. In fact, he always looked forward to the bad guys showing up. Now, he welcomed the postponement. Why?

He didn't have the time to ponder that question, lurking any longer would draw suspicion. Ward continued his way on the landing and walked down a second set of stairs.

Once in his car, he flipped on his cell phone and dialed Brett's number.

"Haynes here."

"I completed a walking surveillance of Ms. Garrett's apartment. Nothing of note."

"Yeah, there was nothing of note when you had me send an agent there last night and again this morning."

Ward held the phone between his shoulder and ear as he buckled his seat belt. "What are you saying?"

"Hey, buddy, I'm not saying a thing."

He snapped the buckle home. "She's a coworker. I practically threw myself on her, and arrested her. I owe her some protection."

"This throwing yourself on her, was this before or after the arresting part?"

Ward revved the engine. Hard. "I'm not dignifying that with an answer."

"One piece of advice."

"What's that?"

"The metal desks don't look as nice, but last longer."

Ward turned off the phone, effectively cutting Brett's laughter. He had no plans of being desked, now or in the future. His friend may have chosen the wife and family route, but that was not in *his* future. He needed the danger. He thrived on the excitement. He'd die sitting behind a desk and sending other men out to do his job.

He tossed the phone to the side, but it ricocheted off a can of frozen concentrate sticking out of the grocery bag. Already the frost was sliding off and dripping onto a package of bagels.

The refrigerator at his own apartment stood bare. The marshals didn't need him to help with Hannah's protection. Why did he have this sense of impending doom? It wasn't just the threat of Kyle Barton. The inklings of a knockdown blow had begun the minute he saw her. And had gone into high gear when he couldn't look away from her with that ice in the break room.

"Ah hell." He pointed the car in the direction of the highway and drove to the safe house.

THE SUN POKED just the barest of rays above the trees as it set. Dusk had always been Hannah's favorite time. Sunset signaled not just the end of the day, but a freedom. Her foster mother once warned nothing good came after midnight. At twelve she didn't understand the sentiment. Once out on her own, she appreciated the full meaning. Embraced it even. After midnight, sex was the only thing to do. In the darkness there were no pointing fingers, no questioning eyes…only fun. At least for a while.

The horizon glowed with the orange, red and purple of the setting sun. The lapping water drew her closer to the lake. An urge to spread her arms wide and run to the boat dock assailed her. But she didn't want to rush it. Then the fine hairs on her neck and arms tightened. She knew without turning Ward was standing behind her. Caught. Heat filled her cheeks. He'd caught her acting out some scene from *The Sound of Music*.

Better get it over with. She turned to face him. Since he looked west, what was left of the sun illuminated his face. His tight features revealed an inner turmoil.

"What's wrong?" she asked, alarm streaking up and down her back.

He shook his head. "Nothing. I've never seen you so…unbound."

Bound. That was the perfect word for her in the office. Bound by regrets, bound by memories, bound by a promise to live. In the dark, a new person emerged. One without guilt, restraints or a past. She'd never shared the freedom of the night with anyone before.

"Walk with me," she invited.

A flicker of an emotion she couldn't define breezed across his face. But like the light wind of the evening, it passed only briefly. His long, roughened fingers curled around hers and he took a step toward her. They turned together, walking deeper into the brush and away from the clearing around the house. He matched his longer stride to hers.

He rubbed his thumb along the back of her hand in an almost absentminded gesture. Her blood heated to liquid fire where his skin touched hers.

A rustling sound and movement in a tree a yard ahead of them broke the spell. Ward grabbed her by the shoulder, pushing her behind him. He drew his weapon and aimed for the tree.

"Get down."

His voice rang cold, like steel.

Nothing happened.

All her senses tuned into Ward. She should be terrified out of her mind, but it was the safest she'd ever felt. She moved closer to Ward's warm back.

He cocked the gun.

The sound sent a small, brown animal scurrying from the limbs and into the shadows of the night.

Ward cursed beneath his breath and lowered his gun.

Hannah's alarm rushed into laughter.

"It's not funny." Ward's voice still carried the cold, hard edge from a moment ago.

"Did you see how scary that little squirrel was? Those teeth!"

Ward uncocked his gun and stuffed it into his shoulder holster.

"Did you see his little whiplash tail? He could have cut us to shreds."

He flashed her an irritated look. "I didn't see you turning down my help by the way you were plastered to my back."

"Are you going to save me from all the wild animals?"

His green gaze was slow meeting hers. "Most of them."

Her smile faded, and a tight, sexual tension replaced her laughter. Her lips parted.

Her movement drew Ward's eyes to her mouth. She sucked in a breath. She leaned closer to him, willing him to kiss her. To yank her hard into his arms. To take—

"Come on. I challenge you to a stone-skipping contest."

She watched as he raced for the dock.

What just happened here?

He'd looked as if he wanted to kiss her. Bad. And now he was the one turning her down. Usually men didn't turn away from her. That had been her power. Her only power.

Shaking her head, she turned. A few moments later, her footsteps on the dock echoed his as she joined him. The wood creaked a bit as she sat beside him. She unlaced her shoes, peeled off her socks and plunged her feet into the cool water of the lake.

But it didn't begin to cool off her desire.

Now.

She should tell him now to leave. That had been the plan. *Follow the plan.*

His stone skipped a pathetic two times.

Hannah reached into his hand. "Give me a rock."

"Your ice is in the freezer."

He threw a stone, but it sank after only one skip.

"Did you get everything you need to stay?"

His stone skipped four times. He shot her a look. She gave him her best impressed smile.

"Enough orange juice to last me a week," he told her, reaching for another stone.

A week. He planned to stay a week. She took a deep breath, and then went with avoidance. "What's this about coffee being undercover work with Protter? Drinking coffee doesn't seem like dangerous, industrial espionage stuff to me."

"All part of the image. Protter expects a tough guy from the résumé I sent him. Ex-Marine, that kind of stuff."

"You mean you aren't an ex-Marine?"

"Yes, I am. I try to keep my undercover life as close to my real life as possible. Fewer mistakes."

"That explains why you had an undercover name so similar to your real one. Ward Cassidy to Ward Coleman."

"Right. What about your name? Hannah Garrett close to your real name?"

She looked back at the water, the rippling waves washing memories closer. "I think of Hannah as my real name. It's the only one I picked out. Someone in the program always did before. I'm going to miss being Hannah Garrett."

"How'd you decide on it?"

"The last safe house I was in had cable. One of the channels played some sort of *Facts of Life* marathon. I watched episode after episode. I liked Mrs. Garrett. The cook on the show. She was a strong, tough woman who knew all the answers and took charge of her own life. I knew all the facts of life, believe me…what I needed was the answers."

"Do you have them?"

She pushed him with her shoulder. He was teasing her. She liked it. "I'm closer. Anyway, when you have about two hours of sleep, naming yourself after an eighties TV show makes sense."

"It makes perfect sense."

"That's when my sleep schedule got off-kilter. Even now I could sleep all day."

"So, you're a night owl?" he asked.

"Definitely a gal of the dark."

"I learned to guard my sleep in the military. My natural inclination is to stay up late, too. But working in the private sector forces me to bed at more reasonable times. The sun will be coming up in a few short hours."

Her rocks gone, Hannah leaned back, her elbows against the dock. "Well, I don't have to go to work tomorrow. Or the day after for that matter. Looks like I'm going to be unemployed for a while."

"I do. Unfortunately my number-one suspect turned out to be a false lead. Come nine o'clock, I start all over again."

"I'd feel sorry for you if my wrist wasn't still sore."

Ward's deep chuckle made her insides swirl. "You didn't tell me how you chose Hannah."

She looked out onto the river. A family of ducks floated by, the mother urging her children on with a quack. "It seemed kind of soft and feminine. I've never felt any of those things."

Ward dropped his rock beside him on the deck and cupped her chin with his fingers. With a gentle pull, he tilted her face to his. She wanted to glance away, but her eyes were drawn to his. As a practice, Hannah shied away from the tender emotions. Tender touches. Tenderness made you want things. Passion was far easier to handle.

He pushed the hair from her forehead and tucked it behind her ear. Tenderness. "You've never seemed anything but feminine to me. And you're soft in all the right places."

The fingers holding her chin drew her close. His lips gave the barest of brushes against hers. She swallowed as his lips traced her top lip, then he sucked her bottom lip into his mouth. She loved it when he did that.

Her nipples tightened at the intimate contact, puckering deliciously against her bra. Liquid heat pooled between her legs. She wanted him. Wanted him closer. Wanted him in her.

Ward nibbled at her bottom lip.

Enough of this half-measure kiss. She wanted passion.

Hannah wrapped her arms around his neck and pulled him to her. Their open mouths met in a desperate, hungry kiss. She sank her fingers into his hair, feeling the strength of his corded neck.

His hands rested at her hips, traced a path up her sides and cupped her aching breasts. A sigh escaped as delicious pinpricks of warmth zapped wherever his fingers skimmed. She arched herself to him, feeling every hard plane of his body.

Her breasts throbbed as his hands left and moved to cup her face. He pulled away from her, resting his chin atop her head.

"I can't."

Her body recoiled from the slap of the cool breeze coming off the water touching her where his body had once been. Hannah had no plans for sleeping alone tonight. She was ready for seduction. She knew his misplaced honor would not allow *him* to take her into his arms. Well, sometimes a woman had to take things into her own hands.

"You can't what?" she asked him. The woodsy, masculine scent of him tickled her nose and made her stomach flutter.

"I can't kiss you."

Hannah placed her lips on his for a quick kiss. He sucked in a breath, but didn't reach for her or return her kiss.

"Tell me what else you can't do."

"I can't touch you."

Reaching for his hand, she placed it on her breast. "Here? You can't touch me here?"

Despite the fact that his hand didn't move, her breasts ached from the warmth seeping from his hand through her blouse.

"What else can't you do?" Her voice had lost its

challenge and become breathy with her growing need for him. Planning seduction was one thing, carrying it out was still another. It had been a while.

"Hannah, what are you doing to me?" His voice sounded tired, yet full of resolve.

She might still have a little work to do. Fantasy Ward was much easier to seduce than reality Ward. He pulled away, and shoved his hands into his pockets. The picture of a frustrated man. A frustrated man not planning to take her up on her invitation. She closed her eyes against the last fading rays of daylight.

"Growing up alone took a lot from you."

Okay. Not what she'd expected. Her eyes drifted open. The group home, or her long-lost foster mother had not been on her mind as his tongue dueled with hers. Or while his hands gently squeezed her breasts. Or as she ran her fingers through his hair. A swift anger chased away her desire.

"What are you talking about?" she asked. Now all she wanted to do was push him into the water. Heck, a cool dousing would work wonders on her own body.

His green gaze was troubled.

"I can't take more from you. You deserve more than a few tumbles before you leave."

Ward braced himself against the wood planking and stood. The wood creaked as he walked to the railing, kicking one of their skipping rocks as he stepped. His shoulders rose and fell with the raggedness of his breathing. He wanted her. Wanted her just as much as she wanted him.

Stooping to pick up the rock, he hurled it out into the

water. A sudden sinking splash and tiny ripples the only testament to his anger.

"I'm here to protect you, that's all."

Without a backward glance, he pushed himself off the railing and headed back to the house. She'd been doing a lot of that lately. Watching this man walk away from her.

Wouldn't he be shocked to know that a few good tumbles before she left may just be what she needed?

11

WARD SHOULD NEVER have looked into her haunting eyes.

What started out as sexual attraction had grown into genuine admiration and more.

Besides the documentation from D.C., he'd also gotten a copy of Hannah's file. The real one. As a kid, she'd bounced around the foster care system, emerging at eighteen with few prospects. No wonder she'd been attracted to the lifestyle a guy like Kyle Barton could provide. Though once she'd seen the truth behind the man, she'd wanted no part of him. He admired her work ethic, taking computer courses, earning her own way in life.

The gravel crunched under his feet as he made his way to the front of the house. He'd heard Hannah enter a few minutes ago. He'd give her some space. He stopped a few yards from the front door. A stone, perfect for skipping rested at his feet. Seeing the stone reminded him of her smile and the revealing words they'd shared. He hunched over and smoothed the rock with his thumb.

The anguish he saw in her eyes at his rejection tore at

his heart. Staying with her at the safe house had been his attempt at apologizing for treating her so badly when he had presumed she was guilty of the money laundering at P&L.

He'd brought this pain to her. And to himself by insisting he stay.

What kind of idiot was he?

Brett was right. He wasn't staying because he felt guilty; he stayed because, pathetic jerk that he was, he wanted to be with her.

He clenched the rock in his hand tight. With a grunt, he hurled it across the lane so hard, the thunk sent a piece of bark flying.

The last thing she needed was him.

And he'd forced himself on her anyway.

The most beautiful desirable woman he'd ever met wanted him, and he had to turn her down. Damn. Damn. Damn.

If he hadn't turned his back on Hannah when he had, he would have reached for her. And then they'd both be in trouble. Because once they'd made love, then where would they be?

Hannah might be content to believe she had a shot at avoiding her inevitable identity change, but he was in the business of facing facts. Men like Kyle Barton didn't give up. In a week, two, tops she'd be gone for good. Gone to a place he could never know or else he'd be putting her very life in jeopardy.

The lawman never got the bad guy and the girl. It never happened.

He'd wait until Jernigan returned, then he'd leave.

He had to. Ward doubted he'd be able to resist the agonizing temptation of Hannah again.

Standing, he made his way back to the clearing around the safe house. Jernigan met him at the door. "Wondered how long it would take for you to make your way back."

Ward pushed his hair off his forehead. "I'm leaving."

Jernigan nodded toward the house. "Finally got too much?"

"Something like that. All she's been through, it's amazing how unscathed she is."

"Hannah's still got a few peculiarities."

Ward nodded. Who didn't have a few? "Good word for it. If I stay much longer, I'll just add to her troubles."

"I kind of thought you were good for her. Let me know when you're going and I'll help you load up your car."

Jernigan might not be so bad. For a marshal.

The light was off in her bedroom. She must have taken an early night. Good. He could slip in while she was asleep. All he needed was to pack.

The last thing he wanted was to see her, and face the temptation all over again.

HANNAH SLOSHED a cube of ice from the glass of pink lemonade. She didn't mind the sweet stickiness of the drink running down her arm cooling her heated skin.

With a flip, she shut off the intrusive light in the bathroom. She'd be able to see just fine with the light from the hallway illuminating the room.

She smoothed the hair off the back of her neck and

ran the cube up and down her nape. Droplets rolled down her back along her spine. Dropping her hair, she ran the cube along her throat. A stream of melted water followed the path of her collarbone and dripped between her breasts. She unbuttoned her top button and rolled the ice along the swell of her breasts.

"Hmm." She couldn't keep the moan from escaping.

A thud outside the bathroom door drew her attention. She turned to see Ward standing in the doorway. His chest rose and fell with the roughness of his breathing. He stood with his hands bracing each side of the door frame. Even in the dim light she saw the look of raw desire on his face.

She wanted him. At this moment, she wanted this man more than anything. Hannah knew how to make a man desire her, to take care of her; none of that was real. But it had always been real with Ward…and he'd rejected her. She raised her hand to cover her exposed skin.

No. She wouldn't hide. If he didn't want to see her body, he could damn well leave.

Once again her fingers went to the buttons of her shirt.

Ward's gaze left her face and followed her movements. Her fingers didn't tremble as she unclasped one button, then moved to the next. When they were all undone, she shrugged out of the cotton shirt. It landed on the bathroom floor with a whoosh.

Ward's Adam's apple moved as he swallowed. His eyes met hers again. The heat in his eyes blazed, but he made no move toward her. She reached behind her back and unhooked her bra. The lace fell to the floor beside her shirt.

Her nipples puckered at the friction of her falling clothes. His pupils dilated, turning the stormy green to a dark, mysterious black.

He shifted, his body blocked the doorway, and she could no longer make out the expression in his eyes. The heat emanating from him filled the bathroom with his musky scent. He stood just a few feet away, yet he made no move to touch her.

She felt no embarrassment or disappointment.

She scooped out a piece of ice and ran it along her dry lips, and he sucked in a breath. Hannah sensed his need. His need for her. She wouldn't let him walk away from her this time. This one night could be her only shot at experiencing the hot passion she so desperately desired. Who knew if Jernigan would bring word of her reassignment tomorrow? Or if Kyle…

Hannah turned, met his eyes in the mirror and began to trace the icy wetness along the line of her collarbone. He groaned behind her. Poor Ward. He didn't stand a chance. She knew it. She reveled in it.

When he moved, he was like a tiger, sleek and coiled, tracking her in the moonlight. His fingers brushed hers as he took the ice from her hand. He wrapped one arm around her waist from behind, pulling her to him. She leaned into his broad chest, closing her eyes for just a moment as the solidness of his body soothed and excited her.

He pushed her hair away from her neck and kissed her skin. With his tongue, Ward licked the sweetness of the lemonade off her shoulder, and her knees buckled. He pulled her tighter against him. Her eyes opened when she felt the hard ridge of his erection against her back.

Her eyes were riveted to their reflection in the mirror above the sink. She watched as Ward's hand moved from her waist to her breast. Shuddered at the sensation. She leaned her head against his shoulder, her eyes drifting shut.

"Don't close your eyes," he whispered in her ear.

Their eyes met and held in the mirror, until he brushed the dripping ice cube to her nipple. The chill of her breast sent heat pooling between her legs.

Hannah watched as he circled the ice around her nipple. A surreal experience, feeling the coldness pucker her flesh as she watched. He moved the ice to her other breast, holding the cube to the already hardened tip while his lips traced the outline of her ear. His arm locked around her waist, drifted lower.

She leaned her head against his shoulder. He urged her legs apart with his knee, and he cupped her through her skirt. She rolled her head from side to side in pleasure, but couldn't resist the urge to look at their reflection.

Ward lowered his lips to kiss the sensitive skin below her ear, his tongue darting out occasionally. She watched as he rolled the ice around her nipple. Saw and felt cool water trail down the curve of her and slide along her rib cage.

The ice against her skin lost its comforting cooling touch. A burning coldness turned her flesh turgid. The bite of the cube froze her skin. She gripped his questing hand. "Ward, I—"

Just when she thought she couldn't take the sharpness of the ice any longer, he shifted, lowered his head and replaced the cube with his mouth.

This time she did close her eyes. Ice and fire warred within her body at his touch.

She sank her fingers into his hair, holding him closer to her breast. "I ache for you, Ward. Don't make me wait."

He glanced up, their gazes meeting once more in the mirror. The drip from the faucet splashing into the sink and the harshness of their breathing were the only sounds in the tiny room. A light wind blew through the window, shifting the curtain allowing more moonlight to stream into the bathroom. The breeze lifted the hair from his forehead. He was rugged, sexy, male and she'd never wanted any man so bad in her life.

She saw the indecision on his face again. Damn his nobleness. Yet it made her desire him even more. If she weren't already crazy with wanting him, that would have sealed the deal.

She reached for his hands. With their gazes still locked together in the mirror she placed one hand on her breast, the other between her legs. Then Hannah smiled. No regrets.

Ward grabbed her hands, and aching disappointment nearly make her scream in frustration, but he didn't pull away. Instead he drew her against the pedestal sink, and positioned her palms flat against the wall. His eyes never left hers.

The hard swell of his erection pushed against her, and she rubbed her backside against his zipper. With a groan, he bunched up her skirt, trapping the material between the sink and her stomach. His fingers traced a path up the bare skin of her thigh. A heated sexual flush spread across her chest.

Ward slid his hand beneath her panties and cupped her. She sucked in a breath when his fingers touched her clitoris. She arched her hips to meet his hand, and her eyes drifted shut for just a moment. But just for a moment, she didn't want to miss anything.

Hooking his leg around hers, Ward spread her legs. His eyes never left hers as he slipped a finger inside her. She moaned, low and deep in her throat as he began to stroke her. Her skin tightened as pleasure coursed through her. Hannah felt weak in the knees yet powerful at the same time. She didn't need to act coy or kittenish or the seductress with Ward. Just the promise of passion hung between them.

And he was making good on the promise. He thrust two fingers into her. She watched the woman in the mirror. Her lips swollen with passion. Her eyes mere slits. The woman before her was having the time of her life, her breath coming out in pants.

Ward's gaze met hers in the mirror. "Watch us," he urged.

His lips trailed along her neck. He sucked her earlobe into his warm mouth, making her crazy. He traced the curve of her ear with his tongue.

She saw the woman grind her body against his. One hand at her breast, the other lost in her panties. She grew slicker around his thrusting fingers. His thumb centered on her clit, teasing her aching nerves. Her eyes drifted shut once more.

"Watch yourself come, Hannah."

His voice was raw and hungry. With effort, she lifted her lids. His thumb flicked her again. Her muscles tensed and she saw what Ward must be seeing in the mirror—an utterly satisfied woman having a mind-blowing orgasm.

Her palms bracing against the wall turned into fists, and she slammed her hips against his. After a moment, her body stopped its quaking.

In one fluid motion he stood, pausing only to dip and lift her up into his arms. He walked down the narrow hallway toward her room.

A strange anxiety loosened the hold desire held on her senses. "Take me to your room."

Ward nodded, backed a step and headed toward his own room. Her momentary apprehension vanished, and she traced the muscles of his neck. The tanned skin beneath her fingers felt on fire. She lifted her lips to kiss his ear.

With a growl, he quickened his pace, kicking the door shut with his foot. In two hurried steps, they were at the bed. He released her knees and she slid down his body to stand before him. The lamp on his bedside table lit the room, and she turned it off, bathing them in moonlight.

Hannah drew his head to hers. She met his lips in a hot, hungry kiss. Their tongues dueled in a quest for closer intimacy. She pulled the soft cotton T-shirt from his pants, running her hands up and down the smoothness of his muscular back.

Ward stepped back, stripping off his shirt and tossing it on the floor. He crushed her to him. His lips found hers, and for a moment, all they did was kiss.

But what a kiss. Her toes curled. Her heart pounded in her chest, and wave after wave of pure desire passed through her body.

She backed up until the bed hit the back of her knees. She lay down, taking Ward with her. Hannah scooted to the headboard with Ward a bare inch behind. His hands found the waistband of her skirt. He unzipped the back and smoothed the light material down her legs.

Ward left her lips to kiss down her neck, over her collarbone and between her breasts. With a light kiss to each nipple, he trailed a path lower with his tongue. He licked the sensitive skin below her breasts. She wadded the sheet between her fingers as he circled her navel and moved still lower until he reached the frustrating barrier of her panties.

His strong fingers pulled her panties over her hips and down past her thighs. She kicked them off to the side. His lips returned to her legs, parting her thighs slightly. The warm wetness of his tongue along the inside of her thigh made her buck.

"Ward, I—"

"Shh."

Just how much was a woman supposed to take? Hannah lay back and scrunched her eyes tight. With an abrupt movement, Ward moved from between her legs and leaned toward the bedside table. She felt a sudden chill. She couldn't let him turn on the light. She reached for his arm but stopped when she heard the ice clink against a glass. *He wanted a drink now?*

"Ward?"

The heat of him warmed her as he joined her again.

"You weren't the only one who wanted some lemonade. Besides, I've had plans for this ice since the heat wave struck, and I saw your favorite cooling method in the break room."

"You saw that?"

"Saw it? Hell, I've dreamed about it."

"What are you going to do?"

His hand pushed at her shoulder. "Lie back down," he told her instead. A cold drip of water landed on her nipple. Ward leaned down to lick it off. He dripped another droplet onto her other breast, but this time he engulfed the entire tip into his mouth. She moaned, arching her back toward him.

He released her and trailed more melting ice water down her body, settling on her stomach. He placed the cube against her belly, rubbing it back and forth. A delicious chill sent warmth flooding right down to her toes.

Ward licked the liquid from her body. "Do you like this?" he asked, his breath tickling her sensitive skin.

"Mmm."

He positioned himself between her legs, spreading them apart. Then he settled the ice cube against the sensitive, hardened flesh of her clitoris.

Sensation after sensation flooded her body, making her clench the muscles of her legs. She dug her heels into the soft mattress. The coldness of the ice cooled her skin and melted against the heat of her flesh. Her chilled skin prickled. She moved side to side, evading the frosty cube.

"Ward, I, uh—"

Just when she didn't think she could take the cold

anymore, Ward replaced the ice with his tongue, sending her spiraling into a chasm of sensation. Wave after wave coursed through her body with each stroke. She flailed her arms, hitting the pillow. She grabbed for it, hugging the softness tight to her breasts, smelling Ward's scent.

Finally, the swells of her orgasm subsided. The bed dipped as Ward moved. He opened and closed the top drawer of his nightstand. She heard him rip the foil packet of a condom and smiled. Ward really was a nice guy. She heard the ice clink against the glass as he got a drink, and then he settled on the bed beside her again.

She expected to feel the smooth glide of his body sliding into hers. Instead she felt the cold shock of ice once again touching her tender flesh. But this time he kept the cube in his mouth. Cold and warmth surrounded her simultaneously and she gasped, looking down at him.

He took the ice out of his mouth and smiled. "Thought I was done with you, huh? Not hardly."

He traced the outline of her with the cube, then held it against her throbbing bud. Once again, the numbing prickle built inside her. She gripped the cotton sheet in her hands. She arched her body to him. She knew this game now. With a groan, he replaced the cube with the long hard heat of him.

She moaned as he filled her with one slow stroke. For a moment, he lay still against her. Her flesh craved the heat of him. Then he moved. A slow, deliberate stroke of his body joining hers.

The slick friction of his body warmed her skin.

Caused her to burn. Where her body once felt boneless, now her muscles tensed. She began to move, meeting him stroke for stroke.

She opened her eyes to look at him. She memorized his raw male beauty as he brought both of them to the height of pleasure. Her eyes drifted shut as a powerful contracting sweetness took over her body. She squeezed him, and he groaned, his strokes becoming less controlled and more abandoned.

With a moan, he pushed into her one more time, the muscles under her fingers bunched. He dropped to her and she welcomed his weight, wrapping her arms and legs about him. She never wanted to forget this moment. Wanted to brand these feelings into her memory forever.

12

WARD WOKE UP holding a pillow. A poor substitute for Hannah, but at least it held her flowery scent.

He rolled onto his back; he felt great all over. Yet he ached for her. The idea of cuddling her awake and then making love had him growing hard.

Where could she have gone?

Tossing the pillow aside, he pulled on his shorts and went in search of her.

Following the bright morning light into the kitchen, all he found was Eric too-free-with-his-first-name Waverly sitting at the table. Waverly lowered his paper. "There's coffee on the stove. Hannah said you liked it strong."

The strange unease he'd felt dissipated, and he hid a smile. The idea that Hannah was messing with him filled him with satisfaction. Crap. He knew he was smiling. They weren't planning to keep the change in their relationship a secret from the marshals, but he didn't have to flaunt it. Smiling like an idiot would be the first thing to go.

"Have you seen Hannah?" Asking the other man anything didn't set well.

"No, I think she's still asleep."

Ward nodded and turned on his heel. Retracing his steps, he found the door to Hannah's room indeed closed. He raised his hand to knock. Waking her up with a kiss had been his last thought before his body surrendered to a sated, exhausted sleep the night before. She'd been pretty worn-out herself. He should let her sleep.

Lowering his arm, he walked into the bathroom and shut the door quietly.

He reached into the stall and turned on the water. It would be nice to take a warm shower for a change. Before meeting Hannah, he hadn't realized that was a luxury.

Why had she left before the morning?

It still stuck—her leaving before he woke her up. Maybe she didn't want to make love to him again. Her satisfied moans still echoed in his mind, scorching his blood. No, it couldn't be that.

His was a strange bed, perhaps she could only sleep in the familiar. He quickly rejected the thought, that couldn't be the answer, either. She had changed identities and homes so many times, attachments to the familiar would have been one of the first things for her to give up if she ever wanted any sleep.

Flashes of her earlier hesitancy, her reluctance to be touched darted across his mind. What was it Jernigan had said? That Hannah had a few peculiarities.

If they hadn't been locked in that elevator, she probably would never have gotten within ten feet of him. It had still taken her days to touch him again.

Trust. Of course it was trust. He should have recognized the signs, she'd floated from one foster home to another, then finally hooked up with a murdering thug, she was on the run, and she'd had more identities than most people had homes in a lifetime. Of course it had taken her a while to touch him.

Why had she? In his own personal sexual torment, he hadn't stopped to think why she wanted to seduce him. And seduce him she had. He hadn't given two thoughts to his investigation since waking up this morning. Bad sign.

Oh, hell. Making love with Hannah while she waited for information about the rest of her life would not jeopardize his ability to focus on his assignment. He could smoke out the culprit behind the scam at Protter and Lane with both eyes closed. James had only sent him here to teach him a lesson before sending him back to the field. To the real danger.

Either he would leave first or Hannah would. They both knew the end was inevitable.

In fact, an affair with Hannah was the safest kind of liaison. No strings and a certain ending. Why hadn't he seen the beauty of the plan before now?

Maybe because he'd been blinded by *her* beauty.

If she wanted to seduce him, who was he to stand in her way?

But yet, there was still something inside Hannah that prevented her from attaining true sensuality. To enjoy touching for no other reason than savoring the texture of a lover's skin. Oh, she knew all about being sensual, but there was a disconnect there. No one ever said he wasn't sensitive.

Tonight he'd show her the pleasures of the senses. Of surrendering in trust. Of tasting the heated passion on your lover's skin. Of seeing your lover flush and yearn for more of your torment. Of closing your eyes and wrapping yourself in the heady scent of passion. Of hearing the sounds of your lover coming undone from your touch alone.

And tonight he'd sleep the whole night through with her in his arms.

With that thought in mind, he shifted the water to cold.

TODAY WAS ONE OF THOSE rare days when everything went right in an investigation. He'd had a breakthrough when he'd scanned a few complaints about P&L from the Better Business Bureau. It had been a long shot when he'd asked them to fax the complaint letter to his apartment, but it paid off. Someone from P&L was sending phony statements to clients.

Small additional bills, in amounts almost unnotice-able. So little in fact, the recipient of the bill most likely wouldn't even investigate and simply pay it. The smallest was less than seven dollars. All bogus. All pure profit to whomever was perpetrating the scam.

He'd started the arduous task this morning of copying the various bills sent out the past month. Next step would be to contact the accounting departments without alerting the perp. He'd start first with govern-ment accounts. Those would be the easiest to obtain.

To make things easier, Protter had been busy all day, so he didn't have to tax himself drinking bitter coffee or making man-talk. The server worked flawlessly—no waiting on reports. The employees seemed to embrace some of the new security measures he'd implemented. Not a single grumble.

Facing little in the way of security work at P&L because of Protter's unavailability, he surreptitiously returned to his initial list of suspects. After removing Hannah's folder, he was left with two potential perps who had access to the mainframe computer, one of which was Protter. The man's file lay on the seat beside him in the car. He'd ask Hannah for her insight on his latest target.

Ward spent the last hour of the day in a state of expectant arousal. That's why he felt like kicking his desk when a special code came over his beeper five minutes before quitting time.

He'd just reported in to Brett this morning. What was so damned important now? He had more important things to attend to, like Hannah's education in the pleasures of all the senses. His desk faced the break room, and whenever anyone opened the freezer for ice his concentration sank.

Hannah.

A new fear, unlike any he'd ever known slammed him into action.

It took only seconds to secure a line, and Brett answered on the second ring.

"Haynes."

"Is everything all right with Hannah?"

"Hannah? What? How would I know?"

A slow aggravation replaced his controlled panic. Aggravation with himself. Shit. It wasn't like him to lose focus. To forget his mission.

A moment of silence hung between the two, only to be broken by Brett's laughter.

"Oh, buddy, you got it bad."

Ward spun his chair and faced the window. The last place he needed to look was the break room. The chirping outside his window had grown louder since last week. The baby birds flourished with each passing day. "Did you have something to report?"

"Oh, so you remember *your* case now?"

Although Brett's words chided, little censure lay behind his question. They both knew Ward was top at his job. The Bureau was his life.

The best possible route to make Brett drop this particular line was to ignore him. He focused on the birds. If he squinted, he could make out the tiny, open beaks of the chicks.

Several long moments passed and then he heard Brett's sigh. "To answer your question, yes, I do have something to report. Noticed a new deposit in one of the offshore accounts."

Ward turned toward his desk and found his pen, all action. This was what he'd been waiting for. They'd considered seizing the account, but Ward had suggested they use it as a trap.

"They don't seem to be on to us. Their paper trail was a little sloppy this time. They're getting confident."

Ward smiled in satisfaction. "Overconfident."

"I've faxed the information to the Gallem satellite office. Look over the paperwork and report back this evening."

"Never any doubt."

"I also faxed all those bills you wanted. There are a lot."

"I live for paperwork, you know," Ward told him dryly.

"You're getting close on this one. James is pleased."

The charged excitement he heard in Brett's voice mirrored his own. Nothing sent his adrenaline surging like the thrill of the hunt. And no one liked it better than Ward. The race was what he lived for.

"One more thing. About Hannah?"

His smile vanished and tension grabbed the muscles of his shoulders. "There's nothing to talk about there."

"Take it from a guy who's been there. You got two choices."

"Oh?" Ward leaned back in his chair, since Brett had come up with one more choice than *he* had.

"You can break it off now, or just enjoy the moment until it's time to say goodbye."

Well hell, those weren't choices. And they weren't any better than anything he'd been able to come up with, either.

"There's no future with this woman if you want to stay at the Bureau. You'd have to join the Witness Protection, too. You'd have to get a real job. You'd have to become anonymous."

That sounded like death.

"Enjoy the moment or say goodbye. But don't get any more involved than you are now unless you're prepared to say bye-bye to your life and all you've worked for."

Ward replaced the receiver and rotated his chair to look out the window again. Mama bird had come with a feast to feed her babies.

His thoughts drifted to his parents, and the vow he'd

made long ago to rid the world of those who preyed on the weak. Like the ones who'd murdered his parents. He might not be going after the kind of street scum he'd always suspected had killed them, but the white-collar criminal could be just as dangerous as the punk on the street. And as deadly.

Ward could never leave the Bureau. It was his life, what he'd trained for since joining the Marines. He was an agent through and through.

Although permanently desked, Brett had managed to get the girl and resolve his case, and stay with the FBI. But Ward would never be so lucky.

Leaving Hannah now was not an alternative, at least not one he wanted to exercise. It stood out as the safest course, but every atom in his body protested loudly at the thought. And when had he ever gone the safe route?

That left enjoying the moment.

He wanted to be with Hannah. Period. His body tightened as he remembered his plans for Hannah tonight. And the next night, and the night after that.

The heat in his veins cooled. Don't look into the future. There wasn't one.

Yeah, enjoy the moment.

WARD CUT THE HEADLIGHTS as his tires crunched on the gravel driveway of the safe house. Going through the paperwork at the satellite office had taken long, frustrating hours. But pieces of the puzzle were falling into place. He'd been able to check off the investment banker as one of his suspects, but added two additional promising possibilities. Both had had access to the mainframe before Hannah was brought in full-time.

Jernigan approached the car as Ward grabbed his briefcase and slid out.

"Evening," Ward called.

The marshal nodded.

"All clear?"

"Nothing to suspect. Anything at the office?"

He slammed the car door shut, scattering a few birds in a nearby tree. "No, everyone seems to buy the story of her having a mild case of the flu. Alert enough to do some work, too, but contagious to visit. Protter's even volunteered to help with some of the server aspects until she can work from the remote here. I've volunteered to bring all the equipment to her."

"Good. Won't draw any suspicion that way."

"Her door remained closed and the clear sensing tape undisturbed."

"Calls?"

"The switchboard forwards them to her voice mail. Traces led only to a few legitimate suppliers, not even a hangup."

"Good."

Ward looked to the front door. "I'm going, to uh, check on Hannah."

The marshal's gaze cut to him.

A classic stare down.

Ward had no intention of backing off. It was none of the marshal's business if his and Hannah's relationship had turned a bit more on the personal side.

Ward almost took a step back when Jernigan's face relaxed into a smile. "You do that. She made cookies."

Turning on his heel, Ward took the steps two at a time. Cookies. The pleasure swirling in him at the thought that Hannah's cookies were because of him was a new emotion.

He almost didn't know what to do first. Find Hannah or find a cookie. Maybe he'd crumble the cookies into crumbs and eat them off her breasts.

Only the darkness greeted him as he turned the knob on the front door. Dropping his briefcase beside the black table lamp, he hurried into the kitchen. He found the platter of cookies on the kitchen table. His stomach instantly rumbled. These weren't just cookies, these cookies had nuts and raisins. He pulled out his notebook and pen. *Buy chocolate chips.* Grabbing a half dozen, he prevented himself from sprinting to her bedroom.

Her closed door stopped his rushed steps. He peeked into his bedroom in the hopes she might be reclining against the pillows. No such luck.

It looked as though he was out of luck. Cookies or no cookies, Hannah's door was closed. And his mama didn't raise her boy to violate an unspoken request. A closed door was a closed door. He stuck a cookie in his mouth instead, and headed for his bedroom. It was late. Hannah deserved a little rest. Hell, he was the one who exhausted her in the first place. *Wipe that smirk off your face.* He stuffed in another cookie as he shut his bedroom door.

HANNAH RELEASED the breath she'd been holding when she heard Ward's door quietly close. Damn. Her earlier twinge of disappointment grew into full-scale frustration.

When she'd heard him approach the door, she'd willed him to knock, sensing his hesitation before going to his own room.

She kicked the covers from her legs. The hot, humid air stifled her. *Damn, damn, damn.* Why couldn't he have just been a normal guy and come in?

Because Ward Cassidy wasn't a normal guy. Look how long it took for her to wear down his resistance.

She heard him flip off his light. The time to act was now. She had no intention of lying in bed all night, craving his touch and doing nothing about it.

Stuffing her feet into her slippers, she opened her bedroom door and quietly knocked on his.

"Come in." His voice rang clear through the door. Didn't he even want to ask who it was?

She smiled as she turned the knob. He knew who it was and didn't want to waste time asking questions he knew the answers to.

A trace of moonlight filtered through his open window. The sheet lowered to his waist as he sat up in bed. Dancing shadows passed along his bare chest. His magnificent bare chest. She sucked in her bottom lip. He was beautiful.

Hannah closed the door behind her and leaned against it. "Hi." She hated that breathless quality her voice had taken. It practically oozed wanting.

"Come closer." Ward extended his hand.

Without hesitation, she walked toward him, only pausing to shut the curtains tight.

She turned and kneeled before him, the mattress dipping under her added weight. With a growl, he folded her into his strong arms. Closing her eyes, she breathed in his musky scent.

"I missed you this morning," he told her before his lips lowered to hers. His kiss was neither tentative nor experimental. Instead it took on the qualities of a practiced lover. A lover who knew how to make her respond.

Her breasts swelled and ached for his lips. The muscles of her legs quivered and warmth soaked her panties. This was what she'd been waiting for. Wrapping her arms around his neck, she met him kiss for kiss, tongue for tongue and nibble for nibble.

She wanted to touch him all over. Her hands lowered and sought his erection. A moan came from both of them as she found his shaft, wrapping her fingers around him.

After a few minutes, his fingers grasped hers in a steel clamp. "Hannah, stop."

His ragged breathing against her neck sent a thrill down to her core. "Why?"

"Because I have plans. I want to invade every one of your senses."

"You've already done that."

"No, different plans." He kissed her nose.

"Interesting plans." He kissed her neck.

"Ones I've been mapping out all day." He kissed her collarbone.

He pulled the T-shirt over her head. Her nipples tightened from the friction of the soft cotton and the picture his erotic words drew.

With gentle hands, he pushed her shoulders downward

until she felt the soft pillow beneath her. Ward leaned forward and kissed each thrusting tip of her breasts.

"You are my blueprint."

"What do you have in mind?" she asked.

Her eyes had adjusted to the darkness in the room, and she saw his lips curl in a smile.

"An invasion. An invasion of the senses. But first, you are wearing too many clothes."

As she only wore her panties, she had to agree. His fingers clutched the material at her hips.

"Close your eyes, Hannah. I want you to lose the sense of sight. Do I need to blindfold you?"

"Maybe," she said with a smile. Her eyes drifted shut at his invitation, and a moment later, the smooth silkiness of his tie covered her eyes. He gently tied it behind her head.

"We're going to enhance your sense of touch. Do you feel my fingers on you?"

"Yes."

"What do you feel?"

Hannah licked her lips and concentrated. "Your fingers are warm against my skin."

He slowly tugged on the material of her panties. The cotton fabric slid easily down her hips. Her breathing shallowed at the erotic sensation of his fingers pushing her clothing down her body. She lifted her bottom to help him remove her underwear altogether.

She expected him to yank down her panties. Wanted him to. Instead he continued with the slow pace. Easing them down her legs, his hands brushing the inside of her thighs. Tantalizing her.

"What do you feel now?"

"You pushing my panties down my legs."

"No. The sensation."

"Everywhere you touch, my skin burns."

"Good. Good."

Ward laughed deep in his throat. The erotic sound sending a shudder through her system. He propped one of her legs up at the knee and pulled her feet out of the material. He did the same with her other leg. Her thighs trembled with his every touch. With skilled fingers he massaged the pads of her feet. Pure heaven.

The bed moved as he shifted to lie on his stomach over her. He hooked her knees on his shoulders and lowered his head.

The warmth from his breath tickled her most sensitive places. She raised her hips closer to his lips.

"I think you need to heighten your sense of touch."

"How?"

"Like this."

In one fluid motion, he lowered his head and gently traced the outline of her with his lips. All sound faded into the background. With the light banished behind the makeshift blindfold, she was all about touch now.

A new powerful sensation flooded her limbs. "Ward, are you humming?"

The vibrations from his mouth to her body nearly sent her over the edge. Her breath came in shallow pants, and her muscles tightened in expectation....

His lips stopped.

She almost cried out in unreleased frustration.

"You're forgetting another sense."

"What?" She managed to croak out the one word.

"Your sense of breath."

"That's not a sense."

He tapped his finger on the softness of her lips. "Just wait. You're holding your breath. You cannot fully appreciate the sensations without your respiration."

"I think I'm doing just fine."

Ward chuckled. Balancing his weight on his knees, he kneeled over her, placing one hand on her belly, the other on her breasts. He caressed her stomach. "Here, you must breathe from here."

He leaned over and kissed her nipples. "Don't breathe from here."

Her eyes still closed, she concentrated on breathing from her abdomen. She'd do just about anything to have him touch her again.

"There you go. Breathe deeply. In and out. In and out."

All this in-and-out talk reduced her to only thinking of his body in hers. Going in and out. Her chest rose and fell with the struggle to breathe deeply. Her stomach clenched in anticipation.

"Why do I need to breathe like this?"

"Because you're about to lose the most important sense of all."

"What's that?"

"You're losing the sense of balance."

When did balance become one of the five senses? Since he had her twisted into knots and her brain like mush, she might have just forgotten.

Ward hopped off the bed and pulled her beside him. "Don't worry about the blindfold. I'll guide you."

Placing her hand in his, she let him take the lead. They didn't make but a few steps.

"I'm going to lean against the wall."

He placed both of her arms around his neck. A rush of tenderness assailed her. She could hug him tight like this forever.

"I want you to put one leg around my waist."

Now this was more like it. She eagerly did as he requested.

"Are you ready for me, Hannah?"

"Yes." She'd die if he didn't enter her now.

He reached between them, guiding the tip of his penis to her welcoming warmth. "You take me," he said.

With a smooth thrust downward, she moaned as he filled her.

"Don't forget to breathe. In and out."

She took two deep breaths, his body expanding within her. The wall of muscles surrounding him trembled.

"Here's where you lose your sense of balance. Place your other leg around my waist and grip me with your thighs."

The soft hair of his thigh tickled her as she quickly moved her leg along his. Driven by complete and total wanting, she gently squeezed him between her legs.

He rewarded her by cupping the soft flesh of her bottom. "Sit back into my hands."

As she settled into his hands, he was able to touch new and different places within her. More warmth flooded her. She nearly screamed.

"Don't forget to breathe, Hannah. As I push in, I

want you to inhale. As I move away from you, breathe out."

He pulled away from her, and she released her breath. As he pushed into her, Hannah inhaled deeply. With each movement her body tightened, and her heart opened.

"Do you feel the wall against your feet?"

"Yes," she told him on an exhale.

"I want you to push your feet against the wall to slide me in and out of you. You decide the rhythm. You decide how deep."

A hesitant push with her feet sent her body into a tailspin of new sensations. She sucked in a breath as gravity pulled her back down again on his shaft. The muscles surrounding him tightened, and she pushed away from him again as she breathed out.

Ward groaned. Smiling she let herself slide down, but not too far. She pushed against the wall again. Experimenting with the depth and rhythm, she teased him into a frenzy.

Whether it was the lack of balance, the deep breaths, or that Ward gave her the keys to their passion, she didn't know or care, but after only two more pushes, her body exploded into a mass of pounding pleasure.

"Ward. Ward, I—"

As if sensing what she needed, Ward pushed into her body again and again. His controlled thrusts of earlier now gone. A new wave of ecstasy filled her body once more, and again when she heard him groan above her.

Ward leaned his forehead against hers. She remembered to breathe. In and out. A small chuckle escaped.

"I must not have done a very good job if you still have energy to laugh."

"Don't worry about your technique. In fact, I was just thinking I'd never be able to breathe again without remembering this."

"You mind if we finish this conversation in bed? I don't think I can stand up like this much longer."

"Wimp."

"Give me about half a day to recuperate, we'll see who's the wimp."

Hannah laughed again.

She unhooked her legs from behind Ward's back. The soles of her feet not quite touching the floor. "Ward, you have to let me go."

"Wait." He dipped and hooked his arm beneath her legs. Swinging her into his arms he took the few paces to the bed and dropped her on the softness of the mattress. He followed, pulling her to him to rest in the curve of his body.

"Mmm. That's better."

WARD'S ALARM CLOCK woke him up again the next morning. It took him a moment to realize why he had this crushing sense of disappointment.

He'd woken up alone. Again.

13

THAT EVENING HANNAH waited for Ward in bed. He'd be late getting back to the safe house. Something about his case. Last night they'd talked about his suspects. She'd offered all she knew, and they'd brainstormed ways a person could get into the mainframe without leaving a trace.

She settled against the pillows in her bed. At least she had the time to catch up on the pirate romance.

The closing of the front door woke her up. Ward was back. She knew it by the goose bumps on her arms. He didn't have to be in the same room with her, and still her body responded in delicious ways.

Hannah sat up in bed, pushing the hair from her face and rubbing her eyes. How long had she been asleep?

She glanced at the glowing red numbers on the bedside clock. After eleven.

The bedroom door beside hers closed.

Hmm. She hadn't even heard him hesitate outside her door.

She pushed the wave of disappointment aside. Poor Ward was ready for bed. Of course, he didn't get the benefit of a nap.

And she didn't plan on letting him get any sleep for quite a little while yet.

Hannah secured her hair in a ponytail and donned her nightgown. White cotton to the floor wasn't exactly the seductive wisps she used to wear, but then she didn't plan on wearing it long.

Smiling as she turned the doorknob, Hannah reviewed the program she had for tonight. Her nipples tightened and a flood of warmth surged through her body as she imagined kissing every sexy spot on his body. Maybe she'd give him an appreciation of a new sense. The sense of breathless anticipation. In and out. *Oh, yeah, she'd been looking forward to this all day.*

After a brief knock, she grasped the cool glass knob and pushed open his door.

Ward didn't sit up in bed as she entered. Had he fallen asleep just as his head hit the pillow?

Hannah licked her lips as images of waking him with a kiss flashed in her mind. When she stood a foot away, Ward abruptly moved, startling her.

"You asked me to take you to my room so you could leave."

His words sounded cold and angry.

She took a step back. "What?"

"That first night we made love, you didn't want to go to your bedroom with me. You said to go to mine. It was so you could leave. Wasn't it?"

Hannah turned away. Anything but to look at him. Anything but to face the burning questions. His and her own.

The springs creaked as he shifted in bed. She expected

to feel his hands on her shoulders any second. But the touch never came.

"Why won't you sleep with me, Hannah?"

The ragged tenderness in his voice nearly drew a sob from her. She wrapped her arms around her middle. Hannah shrugged. "I am sleeping with you."

"You're having sex with me. Don't pretend you don't know what I mean. You said as much that time in the elevator. You're out of here before you're even done coming."

"Don't make this crude."

"You're making this crude. You won't sleep with me, tell me why."

"I can't explain."

"Why? All my secrets are out."

Sputtering irritation made her whirl around. Anger was good. Anger was an emotion she could wrap around herself.

"What secrets? That you're a fed? That one was out a long time ago."

"Don't play those evasion games with me. You know what I'm talking about."

Ward had left the window curtain open, and the moonlight streaming through illuminated every hard plane of his face. Gone were the tender smiles of the lover. Her lover.

"I'll not be used for sex."

Okay, never in her life would she have expected a man to say something like that. Her aggravation with his behavior instantly faded. She lifted her hand to him. "Ward, it's not like that."

"Then what's it like? You tell me."

Her arm dropped. Words would not come.

"Don't come back to me, to my bed until you're ready to sleep with me. Spend the whole night with me. Wake up with me."

Ward turned his back to her.

In silence, she fled to the accepting darkness of her room.

For hours, Hannah tossed and turned between her sheets.

The room beside her lay silent.

Although he probably hadn't realized it, Ward had given her a gift last night. When he'd allowed her to control their lovemaking, he'd unleashed something inside of her. Something totally not sexual. An elemental cleansing.

She took a deep breath. All her senses blazed with a new awareness. Even the clean, country air held a new promise.

A promise Ward had put in her hands last night.

Four years ago, she'd made a vow. A promise of her own. She would never give her trust, the true trust of her heart, to anyone. Anytime she trusted anyone they betrayed her. First her foster mother who hadn't adopted her. The woman who'd raised her for so long had been sick, although she chose not to tell Hannah, instead sending her to live in a group home. And Kyle, his betrayal was of a completely different kind. Because he made her nearly betray herself.

As an adult, she promised never to give another

person the power to hurt her. Her true self. She'd kept that pledge. Was still keeping it.

Ward.

He wanted more from her.

No, he demanded more from her.

He accused her of having secrets. She chuckled at that one. He didn't know the half of it.

He'd leave.

With a certainty burning in her heart, she knew he'd leave, maybe even tomorrow if she didn't share with him everything, not just the safe parts.

Was she ready to have the light of his green eyes brighten the dark secrets hidden in her soul?

Tossing back the covers, she padded to the kitchen. The moonlight reflecting on the still waters of the lake caught her attention. She pushed the curtain aside to get a better look.

She'd taught Ward how to skip stones into that lake.

Skipping stones. Breaking that vow to herself would be like skipping stones. First one skip. The next would skip twice. Then it would be easier.

A handful of days ago, as she stood in the dark of the elevator, Ward had asked if she had anyone waiting for her. There, as she battled fear and fought her self-preservation instinct, she had asked herself if she could trust Ward.

Ultimately, she'd decided she could. And she'd been right to do so. Her body and soul craved the rightness of it now.

Could she trust Ward with her secrets?

Perhaps it was time to make a new promise to

herself. One that pledged she'd grab every chance for happiness life offered her. Actually, she'd already made a step in the direction, going for passion.

The life she'd chosen, the decisions she'd made had left her in pieces.

It was time.

Now was the time to rid herself of the broken parts of her life.

She walked with sure steps to Ward's room. She decided against knocking. He slept anyway.

Hannah pushed the door quietly open and closed it behind her. She braced herself against the hard wood. Ward hadn't closed the curtains after she left so she saw his sleeping male form on the bed clearly.

His back was to her. The sheet hugged his hips. Her fingers curled with an itch to stroke the smoothness of his back.

The beats of her heart multiplied, and every cell of her body was attuned to him.

For a moment, fear warred with her yearning. She could leave now, and he would never know.

But that would be the coward's way. And she would never be a coward again.

In one swift, decisive movement, she tugged her night-gown over her head and let it drop soundlessly to the floor. She took the two steps to his bed and lifted the sheet.

He didn't stir.

She would sleep with him. It wouldn't be about sex. It would be about sharing. For tonight.

Rolling onto the bed, she molded her body to his

broad, warm back. She wrapped her arm about his waist and breathed in his musky scent. Placing a soft kiss between his shoulder blades, Hannah rested her head against the pillow and fell into a dreamless sleep.

WARD WOKE BEFORE his alarm clock sounded. Damn, he hated that. Then he felt her.

A deep, cherishing satisfaction engulfed him. She'd come to him.

And tired fool that he was, he hadn't even woken up to enjoy her slipping in beside him. But by the restful, restored way he felt, he did get something out of it.

Some guard dog he was. But then, even in sleep his body must have known hers and relaxed. The even rise and fall of her breathing let him know she still slept.

In and out. In and out.

His body hardened.

Ward rolled over to wake her with his lips on hers.

But the sight of his beautiful woman made him pause. Her face, usually so troubled, lay relaxed now in sleep. An almost carefree lightness played about her features. He'd spotted glimpses of that sunniness as they skipped stones together on the boat dock. He traced the softness of her cheek. He wondered about the kind of person she would have been without the disappointments she'd faced growing up.

Hannah curled to him in her sleep, and a deep possessive pride took over his desire. Oh, he still wanted her, the growing hardness of his body could attest to that. But now he wanted to discover the woman she was.

He trailed his finger along the paleness of her arm

and along her rib cage. Hannah had no tan lines. She stayed indoors far too much. They were safe here in this house. She could venture out now. Maybe he could convince her to go skinny-dipping in the lake.

She moved her legs, shifting the sheet lower. He slid the rough pad of his finger along the smooth skin of her hip and lower.

That's when he saw it.

He'd felt the scar, knew it was there, but what he saw was so much more. Wave after wave of anguish at seeing the mutilation of her beautiful, innocent body pounded into him.

With controlled movements, he slipped out of bed and pulled on his shorts. Closing the door quietly behind him, he made his way outside and in search of Jernigan.

He found the man inspecting the seal of the windows on the north side of the house. He looked up as Ward approached.

"What happened to Hannah's leg?"

14

"I ASKED YOU A QUESTION. What happened to her leg?"

Jernigan looked away.

Rage boiled up inside Ward. He wanted to hit somebody. Anybody. He'd hate for the marshals to bear the brunt of his fury at Kyle Barton, so he turned away from the man he'd grown to respect these last few days.

Ward bent and grabbed a handful of rocks from the gravel driveway and flung them as hard as he could. The cracking sound of bark and the surprised caws of disturbed birds filled the air, then silence fell.

He'd learned more of Kyle Barton, had done some research on the Internet during downtime at his office. The guy was a nutcase. A dangerous nutcase, and someone best locked safely behind bars forever.

A nutcase roaming around loose right now.

He returned his attention to Jernigan, and raised an eyebrow.

The marshal shook his head. "This is something Hannah should tell you."

"Do you know how long it's taken just to get into a position to *see* what's on her leg? The last thing I'm going to do is ask her about it, make her relive it."

His stomach twisted. He couldn't erase the image of Hannah's mutilated skin. He'd seen gunshot wounds before, he knew what they looked like, but this...this was something else.

He raked his fingers through his hair. "Hell, she might think I already know."

Ward grabbed another handful of rocks and hurled them down the driveway. He'd spare the poor birds the disruption.

Jernigan hunched down to the road and grabbed a few rocks and joined him. "I've never seen the damage to her leg, but I knew it was there. The psychiatrist listed it in her report."

Rubbing his eyes, Ward tried to block the image of the slash marks running up and down her thigh.

"So many things make sense now. The long skirts and pants, even when it was a million degrees outside." *Why she came to him only at night.*

"What I don't understand is why. There was no mention of this in the official reports."

Jernigan tossed another rock, almost making it to the leaning remains of the mailbox. "It was at her request. Once Kyle realized he couldn't control her, he toyed with her a bit, before he planned to kill her."

Ward's stomach clenched at the sick reason behind the damage done to her body. He wanted to throw up. Barton better hope someone caught him before Ward found him.

"Bleeding, she managed to escape. That's when they shot her, but on she ran."

Good girl.

The two walked in silence, the morning sun already heating the air.

"Surely with some reconstructive surgery, they could have smoothed out the damage. That's one hell of an identifying mark."

"Hannah didn't want them to. Said she wanted to carry it around as a reminder of a promise. A promise of what, she never told us. The psychiatrist stressed it would be best to have it removed, but she was steadfast."

"Damn. Sometimes her strength astounds me."

Jernigan nodded. Something prickled on the back of his neck, and Ward turned toward the house. Hannah stood in the window, watching them.

His heart ached at the sight of the beautiful woman who'd gifted him with her trust somewhere in the wee hours of the morning light. For some, trust was easy to give, but he knew Hannah kept hers closely guarded. His chest swelled, and he took a deep breath. He hadn't realized it at the time, but now he felt as if he'd won some hard-fought battle.

"Time to get ready for work."

"Wait."

Something in Jernigan's voice made him pause from his sole intention of returning to Hannah and wrapping her in his arms. He turned and looked at the other man.

"I've never seen Hannah like this before. It's a good thing, I think. But Cassidy, you gotta know this has to end. I don't get involved with the people I protect, but in this case, I don't want to see Hannah hurt. Think about that before it gets too out of hand."

He almost told the marshal to mind his own damn business. His muscles tensed, and he dug his heels into the gravel drive. Then he thought of Hannah.

They both wanted to protect her. And why was he so ticked at Jernigan anyway? He hadn't said anything different from Brett. Hadn't echoed anything that wasn't already swirling with accusation in his subconscious.

"I'll do that."

WHEN HE ARRIVED AT WORK, he found the back door of Protter and Lane had been propped open with a folded piece of cardboard, and several computer monitors stolen.

He pegged the culprits as petty criminals, and the crime more that of opportunity than careful planning. But now he had the ammunition to convince Protter of the merits of a door alarm system.

He'd planned to work on the invoices. While reviewing the ones Brett had faxed, he'd noticed what the government thought they'd paid did not match what P&L recorded. In fact, every amount had been rounded down to the nearest tenth. On the surface, it wouldn't appear like a lot of money, but over time, and with the kind of large accounts P&L dealt with, the money would add up.

Instead, his investigation into the computer thefts, conversations with the police and his various reports had him working long past the five o'clock quitting time. When he realized P&L did not keep a record of the serial numbers of all their equipment, he knew he had a new and large project on his hands.

He was an agent with the FBI, not a damned security chief. But his conscience wouldn't let him turn his back on such a mess.

The sun was low on the horizon as he took the elevator down to the parking garage. The fan in the ceiling kicked on, lifting some of the humidity from the elevator car. He remembered the last time he'd felt the hot, damp air in this tiny box…and his means to relieve it. Damn. He hadn't been able to get into an elevator in this building without thinking of Hannah naked in the dark.

He loosened his tie as he shut the car door. Protter had deemed the office air conditioner sufficient once again and casual days were banished back to a distant dream.

Traffic out of the downtown area was light this time of night. Driving around and listening to music would help him shake off the tensions of the day. The business district of Gallem had undergone a revitalization of sorts the last few years. New trees and lighted arbors and topiary gardens made the warehouses and sky-scrapers less steel and glass and more human.

Protter had given him several files for Hannah to scan. Yeah, as if she'd be working tonight. Protter's files could wait. He couldn't. Besides, the way things were looking, the least of Protter's worries should be the files. Maybe Dan should start thinking about a good criminal attorney. On the surface, it didn't seem likely the man would steal from his own company. Since P&L wasn't publicly traded, he could enjoy his profits to the fullest.

He went over and over just what Protter's motivations could be until he pulled into the rutted driveway of the safe house.

Ward found the house dark and quiet. Walking to his bedroom, he pulled the tie from his collar. He hated the things, but when he'd traded in his Marine fatigues for a name badge at the FBI, the tie had come with the package. His brief tie reprieve at P&L didn't make him miss tying a knot around his neck any less. Unbuttoning his shirt, he quickly changed into shorts and a T-shirt.

As he suspected, Hannah's door was closed, and no light peeked from under the door.

The dock.

The adrenaline pumping through his veins made him forget his exhaustion. He passed Waverly on his way outside. The younger man flashed him a look full of resentment before he masked it. It dawned on him that maybe the marshal had a slight crush on Hannah. Well, he couldn't fault the kid for taste, but he needed to keep his eyes and his first name to himself. With a curt nod to him, Ward stepped out into the night.

With the sun now fully set and a light breeze in the air, the evening had turned almost pleasant. It took only moments for his eyes to adjust to the darkness.

Hannah leaned against one of the railings of the dock, her red hair loose and blowing in the breeze. Two mounds of rocks piled beside her. The one closest to her stacked lower than the other. How long had she been waiting for him?

She sat a little straighter. He'd been quiet in his approach—she hadn't heard him.

She picked up another stone and tossed it into the water, resulting in a pathetic three skips. Pretty good for him, but pitiful for her.

Pulling off his tennis shoes, he sat down beside her and plunged his feet into the green water of the lake. He'd never been one for mucking around in dirty water. He'd had plenty of that as a Marine. But letting the gentle current of the water massage his feet at the end of the day had become a pleasure he planned to continue. Although he probably would never be able to pull it off without thinking of Hannah.

Pain stabbed his heart at the mere thought of a future without Hannah. Enjoying the moment had its drawbacks.

Ward picked up a rock and tossed. Four skips. Pretty good. He didn't know how long they sat in silence, skipping rocks, but soon her pile was gone and she began to reach into his, their fingers brushing by accident.

If she wasn't going to start the conversation, then he would. "I could wake up with you like that every morning. I don't know why, but I know that was hard for you to do."

Just when he thought they'd spend the evening in silence, she cleared her throat, "I don't want you to see me in the light." The words came out rushed.

He understood. Relief swamped him, and his stone nearly skipped five times. "Hannah, if it's about your leg, I saw the scars."

She sucked in a breath. "No, it's not that. I mean, it is that, but that's not the reason why…."

Her words trailed off.

The nervous timbre in her voice made him ache. As Hannah reached for another of his stones, he turned to her, stilling her hands in his.

"Tell me," he urged.

Her gaze lifted briefly to his, then she squeezed her eyes shut. He counted ten beats before she opened them again.

"It's the light. I don't like to be touched in the light." She pulled her hands from his and turned away again.

Hannah's shoulders bunched and she drew her knees closer.

He knew what was wrong. She was bracing herself for some kind of rejection or rebuke. Anger stirred deep. He wanted to wrap his hands around the person that did this to her.

With gentle fingers, he brushed the hair from her face and tucked it behind her ear. He wanted to see her better. "I've touched you plenty of times in the daylight."

She shook her head. "No, you haven't. Think about it, Ward. We've been together in an elevator, and in your bedroom, both in the evening."

"This morning—"

"This morning when I slipped into bed with you, I tried to battle my demons. I wanted to touch you this morning, to be *able* to touch you, ached to do so. I certainly never had a problem in the past touching a man, light, day, whatever. But that was before…"

"Before what?" he urged.

She turned her head away, but he didn't press. He knew she would answer. He glanced out onto the lake.

Mama duck paddled with her young in the distance. "I've not been with a man since Kyle. I haven't really trusted myself since then."

"Why?"

"What kind of woman is drawn to an evil man like that?"

Ward shook his head. "You didn't know."

"I knew something wasn't right, and I didn't question it. In fact, I liked the way he'd shower me with designer clothes, the rock of an engagement ring he gave me. We drove expensive sports cars and lived in an amazing apartment, but I never saw him really work. I just blissfully accepted his vague explanation about an inheritance. And you know why? Because I liked it. Because I liked being the sexy girlfriend of a rich and powerful man."

At eighteen Hannah had nothing. When Ward turned seventeen, he was burying his parents. They both bore the brunt of pain at a young age. Before his parents' death, he'd been a hopeful kid. Hannah had lost any chance of being a kid. "You grew up with nothing, it's understandable that you were seduced by it all."

"Kyle understood things about me, could look into my soul. That's why he always seems to find me. He told me we were connected. I could never lose him. He said it slow, like those persuasive voices the psychiatrists use when they put you under hypnosis."

She turned away from him then, and he felt he'd lost a huge battle. "He told me he would consume me. Take everything until we were one."

Bitter anger grew inside his heart. Kyle had achieved

exactly what he wanted. The idiot stood between them now. Jernigan's words echoed in his mind. At times she was both fragile and the strongest woman he'd ever seen. He wanted to remind her of that strength now.

"Tell me about the night you got away from him."

"I'd surprised him. I followed him one day, I wanted to see what he did when he was gone. I don't know why, it was stupid really. Instead I stumbled into Kyle's multimillion dollar bookmaking operation. He'd just murdered someone. And I was just supposed to accept it, pretend I didn't see it. I couldn't. I started to run. When he caught me…it wasn't good." Hannah's hand reached for her leg.

"I knew he was going to kill me. Kyle could be cruel."

It took all the strength of his will not to clench his fist. The thought of that animal touching Hannah, his Hannah, put him in a fighting mood.

"I found another opportunity to make a break for it."

"But you were caught."

"By one of Kyle's associates. Jim. Only he was really an operative for the government. He helped me escape. He put his life on the line for me. He died helping me."

To his utter surprise, Hannah lowered her head into her hands. Deep, racking sobs quaked through her entire body. For a minute, he didn't know what to do. Crying women were one thing, but a woman like Hannah, filled with so much pain, and expressing the blows to her soul, was very different.

Instinct took over. He pulled her to him, cradling her head to his chest. Ward didn't know how long he held her next to him, but nothing had ever felt so right.

As the moon lowered, her tears subsided.

"You know I've never cried. Not once. Not when my foster mother didn't want me. Not when Kyle hurt me. Not when he found me the first time. Tears are weak."

He cupped her face, and kissed a tear away from her cheek. "You are never weak. You're one of the strongest people I've ever met."

She glanced away, and he felt her physically and mentally pulling away from him. Everything male and protective inside of him shouted in protest. He kissed the tip of her nose, gaining her attention.

"I'm not strong. I can't even let you touch me in the light. In the light I have to see who I really am. Who I really was."

"It will come."

"I don't really like the person I was then. Sometimes that woman seems a lifetime ago, but she's still right there, always a part of me. Look how easy it was for me to turn on the sex appeal, to try to seduce you. Those were the weapons I used to have."

He was beginning to see her logic. "That's why you turned it off. If a sexy woman draws someone like Kyle Barton, then you wouldn't want to be a sexy woman."

He handed her a stone, his last, and she tossed it into the lake water. No skips. "That's right."

"But you are sexy, Hannah. Sexy as hell. You turn me on like no one else. And what do you want from me?"

"What do you mean?"

"Are you trying to distract me from doing my job?"

"No."

"Trying to get some special favor?"

"No."

"In fact, when you knew I suspected you of something, you didn't lay out the sexy appeal."

"No, I almost pulled out my Taser."

He laughed. "Yes, that's right. What do you want from me?"

"Pleasure."

"To give and receive."

A smile tugged at her lips. "You know, putting it that way, it doesn't sound half-bad."

Suddenly he became a man on a mission. Before she left for her new identity, he wanted Hannah to break the spell Kyle still held over her. The best way he knew to do it was for her to enjoy lovemaking in the daylight.

"How does it feel when I touch you in the dark?"

He traced the curve of her jaw with his finger. She leaned into his caress.

"Mmm. Heavenly."

Ward traced the delicate line of her collarbone, her skin soft and warm beneath the roughness of his finger. "Think of the way this feels. When I touch you here tomorrow morning."

Her hand blocked the movement of his questing finger. "No, Ward, I don't want to risk it."

"Risk what?"

"Risk losing what we have now. It means too much to me."

His heart swelled at her declaration. Their brief time together meant as much to her as it did to him.

"Will you trust me?" Ward took a deep breath. He'd been asking her to do that a lot lately.

"I want to."

"It's not a question of wanting. You've got to *make* yourself, Hannah. Will you trust me?"

He felt a slight tremor pass throughout her body. Preparing himself for rejection, he steeled his nerves. Hannah had been through so much, maybe he pushed too hard. Maybe now was not the right time.

She put her hand in his. "Yes."

It took everything calm and controlled inside him not to grab her, spin her around and then race to the bedroom with her over his shoulder firefighter style.

Instead he tipped her chin and placed a gentle kiss to her tremulous lips. His hands ached to mold her breasts. *Hey, you're with the FBI, you pride yourself on cool patience and resolve.*

"Feel my lips on yours? Do you want more?"

Hannah wrapped her arm around his neck and drew his mouth closer. "I ache for more," she said against his lips.

Her warm breath against his mouth shot red-hot desire straight to his penis.

"What about my hands here?" He trailed soft fingertips down her sides to cup her rounded hips.

"I want you to touch me everywhere." Hannah pressed hard against him, her breasts crushing into his chest.

Steeling himself for what he had to do next, he reached behind him and pulled her arms from around his neck.

He stood, brushing his hands against his legs. "We'll start tomorrow morning."

Her confused and hurt expression nearly made him yield. But if this were to really work, she needed to trust herself enough to come to him in the daylight. Not wake up that way after reveling in the night.

Ward extended his hand and helped her to her feet. Leaning forward, he kissed her lips tenderly. After a moment, they both panted with ragged breaths.

"It will be the same tomorrow morning. Remember that. Concentrate on that."

She looked toward the house. "Are you coming?"

"No, I told the marshals I'd take a shift tonight."

With a nod she turned and headed for the house. He watched her until she mounted the steps and closed the door behind her.

Damn. He was probably in for another cold shower tonight.

But, oh, tomorrow morning.

15

HANNAH HAD SET HER ALARM, but she'd awoken long before dawn anyway. In just a few minutes, she was going to walk into Ward's room, strip off her robe in front of him and lie down beside him. In the light.

Delicious thrills and nervous tension battled within her. How was she going to do it? How could she not?

Already the morning light peeked through a slit in the curtain. Climbing out of bed, she followed the light to the window.

She closed her eyes from the brightness. For a moment, she allowed the sun to hit her.

"Good morning."

The curtain slipped from her fingers as she turned. Ward stood in the doorway, dressed in a shirt and slacks and tie. She tamped down her disappointment.

"Why are you already dressed for work?"

"The offshore bank is finally handing over their documents on the accounts. I think I'll have enough evidence for a subpoena. Make arrests this weekend. Besides, all the tossing and turning from this room kept me up all night. I figured I might as well go into work and search for the bad guy," he said with a wink.

His tone was light, but she sensed the tension in him. Walking toward Ward, her heartbeat increased. How was it that she could have been so intimate with this man, shared some of her darkest secrets yet seeing him at her door still made her heart jerk? The man had seen her at her very worst. And her worst was scarier than most people's.

When only inches separated them, she reached up and straightened his tie. Her unconscious move was so natural, yet her hands still shook. She clasped them behind her back.

Ward didn't seem to notice. He nodded toward the window. "It's daylight."

She nodded. *Let it fall.* All she had to do was let her robe fall to the ground. She willed herself to do it. In the dark she could do anything, was fearless, but here…

Shaking her hand to loosen her fisted fingers, she reached out and grasped the terry cloth edges of her robe. All she had to do was tug at the belt and shrug the material off her shoulders. Easy breezy. She balled the material in her hand.

How was she going to be with Ward if she couldn't drop her robe?

With dark resolve, she grasped the belt and let the robe fall, pooling at her feet. She stood before him naked, nearly naked. Her panties still hugged her hips.

Ward sucked in a breath, the green of his eyes darkening and she felt his gaze skim along her body like a caress. "How did that feel?" he asked.

She swallowed the large lump in her throat. "Taking

off my robe felt great. It was the buildup that nearly killed me."

Ward laughed deep in his chest. "Remember that."

With a quick kiss to her cheek, he reached for her hand and drew her toward him. "This is the hardest thing I've ever had to say, but walk me to my car."

"We're not going to, uh…" Why did she have to stammer like an idiot? Only days ago she'd had him pinned against the wall, buried deep inside her.

"We'll take one step at a time," he said, picking up her robe and slipping it over her shoulder.

Her steps slowed, and she hesitated as he drew her near the front door. He *really* did want her to walk him to his car. Her blood rushed again, and a small headache began to form behind her eyes.

What was wrong with her?

But she knew what was wrong with her. Going outside with Ward right now meant something very different. She'd be acknowledging a relationship. It meant she was ready to give up the fear. Or at least it meant maybe she was ready to at least face the fear. Ward pushed the screen door open ahead of him, and she walked out onto the steps. She closed her eyes and let the sun warm her face again.

But Ward wouldn't let her dwell. He reached for her, and they walked, hand in hand, to his car.

He kissed her lightly on the lips.

"A man could get used to this."

She leaned against him, and drew his head down to her lips. Tracing the outline of his mouth with her tongue, she finished her assault with a deep, long kiss.

"Have a good morning," she said.

His expression looked pleasantly pained. "It's going to be some kind of morning all right."

She laughed and watched him back out of the driveway and zoom off to Gallem.

Hannah retraced their path back to the safe house. This morning did feel good. She felt somehow lighter.

He'd said he could get used to this.

No, he'd actually said a man could get used to this. Well, her kind of woman *couldn't* get used to it. It was pretend.

They were both here on borrowed time. Ward was only in Gallem until he solved his case. She didn't even know where he really lived. And she…well, she was only here long enough for them to find Kyle or find her a new location.

But she could pretend while they were both here. She was really good at that. She could pretend anything.

As she walked up the steps, a patch of pink caught the corner of her eye. With a gasp of delight, she retreated down the steps and tiptoed her way through the brush surrounding the house.

WARD PULLED INTO the gravel driveway later that evening to find both the marshals outside. With Hannah.

Her eyes glowed, and her cheeks were pink. Even the tip of her nose had reddened. From the sun?

"What is she doing?" he asked Jernigan.

"She's been out here all day."

"Oh, Ward. I'm glad you're home. Look what I found outside."

He smiled at the excitement in her voice. He'd never seen her like this before. For once she looked like a person ready for the life ahead of her, not one weighed down by the past.

Tugging at his tie, he hunched down beside her.

"Look at these beautiful flowers. I love the pink ones, those are what I spotted first."

Ward noticed the clearing she'd made in the flower beds in front of the house. He hadn't even realized the beds existed hidden under so much overgrown brush. She'd made two large piles of weeds and debris, and she must have been at it all day.

He hated to see all her work go to waste. The delicate pink flowers didn't look as if they could withstand the hundred-plus weather. "Those flowers might die out here in this hot sun."

She looked up and scratched her chin, leaving a dirt smudge across her face. Pain shot through to his groin. He wanted her right now.

"No, they won't. These are vincas. They thrive in hot weather and full sun. Make sure they have enough water, and they're good to go. As soon as I sent you on your way, I saw these pink petals and knew I had to rescue them."

Yeah, sent him on his way. Hell, he hadn't been able to think of anything but that kiss all day.

"These flower beds extend all around the house. There's even a vegetable garden in the back. It would be lovely to grow some vegetables."

Sounded like roots. He'd read Hannah's files; she wasn't a woman who put down roots, before or after

Kyle. He stroked the petal of the nearest vinca. Not much of a scent, but the beauty of the flower hid a sturdy stalk.

"They grow from seed. They've probably been growing wild out here every summer, just waiting for someone to give them a little tender loving care."

He was in need of some tender loving care. Dirt-covered and exuberant, Hannah had never looked lovelier.

He saw the hope in her. She'd finally begun to believe that she could go back to work and her apartment, and all would go back to the way it was before Kyle escaped.

That's why Ward approached her with a heavy heart.

She'd sunk her fingers into the dirt. "I found some bulbs, too. Bet we'll have daffodils next spring.

The sign they'd been waiting for and dreading had come. Inquiries. Someone was making subtle inquiries into Hannah Garrett.

She turned as Ward's body cast a shadow across her face. Hannah smiled at him; the familiar pull between them tempted him to tell her later. Much later.

Her lips trembled a bit when he didn't return her smile. She shook her head. "No."

Amazed at how words ceased to be needed between them, he simply nodded.

The previous joy on her face turned to anguish. His heart ached to see her pain.

"No. Damn it, no." She tugged at his pant leg, grinding dirt into the cuff. She pulled him down beside her.

"The computer blipped today. Someone's searching you out."

"Which name?"

"The current. Hannah Garrett."

Hannah turned away from him. She reached for a small weed growing beside a white vinca. She stabbed at it with her digging tool, then ripped it from the dirt.

"And Kyle?"

"Still no sign of him yet."

"There won't be until he's sure. When do I start learning my new identity?"

"It might not come to that. A new agent is coming by tonight for a briefing."

"Let's not kid ourselves, Ward. That's why we're here anyway. For me to put Hannah behind me. This last week, what we've had here…it was a bonus."

He reached for her shoulder, pulling her to him and kissed her. Her lips remained cold and unresponsive beneath his.

His hands fell to his sides, and she turned away from him. She reached for the petal of the pink vinca, the first flower she'd pointed out to him.

With a guttural wail, she grabbed the vinca by the stem and wrenched it from the earth. Dirt flew from the roots and scattered about them.

Ward watched helplessly as she pulled flower after flower from the bed. He needed to fix this for her. He needed to make this right for her.

Finally exhausted, she rested. Her head hung low; her chest rose and fell heavily from her efforts. Dirt smudged her arms and face.

The sound of the wind rustling the leaves on the trees

and the lonely call of the locusts filled the air. Everything inside him said to comfort her. But he knew it would do no good. Hannah was back in a place he could not touch.

"I'm sorry, Hannah."

"Don't call me that. It's not my name."

She peeled off her gardening gloves and threw them beside the mess of flowers and dirt. Without looking back, she mounted the steps, and went inside.

"Hannah, I promise you, if it's the last thing I do, I'll hunt him down."

AFTER TAKING A SHOWER, she stayed in her room all afternoon with the curtain drawn tight. No tears would come. This was just her life. Why waste tears on something she couldn't change? She already was aching for the touch she knew she could never feel again.

Ward's touch.

Why had he kissed her today? If he'd just told her the news and left, her body and soul would not be yearning for his comfort now.

She hugged the pillow tight to her chest. Why had she let herself fall for Ward? Why had she slept with him night after night?

Hadn't she told herself it was pretend? That leaving and never seeing him again *was* the most likely outcome? But yet she still hoped. Damn. Hope had been the one thing Kyle hadn't successfully taken from her.

She'd done that one all by herself.

He would leave now. The rustling sounds coming

from the room next door sounded as if he was packing. Packing to leave her. The agony of it twisted in her heart.

The unfairness of it all hit her. Why was she in bed hugging a damn pillow when she could be touching Ward one last time? She'd wasted enough time in her life running away. Now she wanted to grab for the last few moments of pleasure and happiness. Tomorrow and the day after were sure to be lonely. Tonight, now, didn't have to be.

Shucking the sheets tangling around her legs she padded to his room.

She found his door open. Ward stood organizing a stack of pants. He'd taken off his shirt and tie. His slacks hung loose on his slim hips. The soft light cast shadows across the hard planes of his stomach and the strength of his arms.

He was so handsome.

Drawn to his skin, she stroked his shoulder, placing a kiss on his back.

He turned, reaching for her. "I have to go," he said above her ear. All the while his arms tightened around her.

"Not yet. Stay until I have to leave."

He shook his head. "I can't. My presence would just remind you of your…old life. You need to concentrate on what's to come."

"I don't care about what's to come. I want now."

"*I* care, Hannah. You gotta do this right. You can't let that nutcase catch you."

"Then stay until the new agent arrives. Just until then."

He closed his eyes. She saw the battle of emotions within him. The arms holding her tightening.

Deciding to pull her advantage, she kissed him on the chest. Loving the feel of his hair-roughened skin, breathing in his musky scent.

"Hannah, I lo—"

"St-stop." Her heart broke at that moment. When the tears would not come earlier, they threatened now. She blinked several times and turned her back to him.

An awkward silence stretched between them. It was already starting.

It would grow only worse because she knew she wouldn't be able to say the words back. They couldn't come. "You can't."

"Why not. Tell me, Hannah."

She whirled around to face him. "I don't want to fall in love. I don't want to find a soul mate. I don't want…"

"You don't want what?"

"I don't want to *want*. When I want, it goes. My foster mother, my homes. The Program is just more of the same. It's dangerous. You're dangerous."

"How am I dangerous to you?"

"Because you make me want," she told him, her hands an agitated mess at her sides.

He reached for her hands, stilling their movement. "Then I'll wait."

And just like that it was over and so easy. She didn't have to give him the words and it didn't stand between them anymore.

"Then make love to me, Ward."

Without a moment's hesitation, Ward pulled her into his arms, then laid her gently across the bed. His fingers went to the top button of her shirt.

"Turn off the light."

He looked up, and their eyes met. Despite the fact that she'd made huge strides in her forays into the daylight, sex in the light had eluded her.

Pain flashed in his eyes, and for a minute she almost thought he'd refuse. Then with a tight nod, he reached for the switch, plunging them into darkness.

Wrapping her arms around his neck, she drew him down to her. Their lips met in a bittersweet kiss of sadness, love and lost hope.

They'd been together every way she thought possible, but tonight Ward simply held her in his arms and gently kissed and stroked her body. His tender fingers moved her legs apart, and with a slow, loving touch he entered her.

They lay joined together. Not moving.

Emotion after emotion surged through her body, sending her to topple over the brink. Her muscles clamped the heated length of him, and he began to move within her.

She arched toward him. She could never get enough of this man.

Tonight, he truly made love to her.

Tomorrow, he would be gone.

16

HANNAH WRAPPED THE SHEET around her and stared at the ceiling. Her body felt deliciously languid, but inside her heart ached with pain of her failure. Once again.

These were their last moments together. Ward practically told her he loved her. And she so yearned to tell him…to tell him what?

She pounded the pillow a few times, then rolled it under her head. The feelings she had were so much more than just plain love. Her foster mother had said she loved her. Kyle had said he loved her.

But with Ward…she knew his love was real. True.

Was she ready to accept it? Could she even?

She rolled over and snuggled to Ward's pillow. The cotton felt cool beneath her cheek. He'd left his bedroom at least fifteen minutes ago to meet with the marshals and the new agent. She hoped her next relocation wouldn't be as hot as Gallem. She smiled. Of course, if it hadn't been so hot, she and Ward wouldn't have stripped to the bare essentials in the elevator.

And she would have missed the most incredible week of her life.

Little more than whispers, the men's voices drifted

in from the front room. They were probably wondering where she was.

She reached for her robe. She couldn't delay the inevitable much longer. The voices outside became angrier as she stepped into the hallway.

She'd zip into her room and put on slacks and a top.

"That's ridiculous. You'd be throwing away your whole career."

Hannah stopped midstep.

"Some things are more important than a career. I have some time away. I want to see Hannah installed safely."

"That's *our* job," Waverly said.

"You'd blow her whole cover."

Her knees wobbled, and she stopped herself from gasping.

No. It couldn't be his voice. He was dead. He'd died four years ago. Saving her.

Taking a deep breath, she forced her legs to walk down the hallway and into the living room. Leaning against the wall, she angled her head to get a better view.

Ward stood with his back to the three men. His stance wide, his hands at his side, his whole body exuded his readiness to do battle.

Waverly and Jernigan flanked him.

The man sitting on the couch drew her eyes. The lamplight made his bright blond hair shine like golden rays of sun. She shook her head. No. He was dead.

The new arrival looked up, his head turning in her direction. She tried to duck into the shadows, but stunned surprise locked her bare feet to the linoleum.

No, it wasn't him.

He stood. The skin around his eyes pulled tight, his face a web of hard lines. But he wasn't as old as she remembered.

She took a step backward, shaking her head.

The man raised a hand to her. "Sarah?"

The sound of her name, her real name, caused a wave of emotion to bubble through her. In a flash, her shock subsided, swells of unexpected joy cast clear through to her heart.

"Jim?" Her voice breaking, she ran into his arms. She hugged him tight.

The man she held shifted slightly, his arms coming slowly around her shoulders in a slow, awkward hug.

Hannah pulled away to look up into his familiar face. She ran her fingers along his jaw, the stubble prickled her skin.

"How can this be? How can you be here?"

He gently steered her to the couch.

"Can someone tell me what the hell is going on?" Ward's angry, confused voice broke her from the spell of seeing Jim again.

He stalked toward her, placing his hand on her shoulder. "Who the hell is this guy? I thought you were here to give Hannah her assignment."

She placed her hand on Ward's. "Ward, this is Jim. The man I told you about. He saved my life when I escaped from Kyle."

"I thought you said he was dead."

She turned to her former rescuer. "I thought so, too. How can this be?"

Jim flashed her a tired, almost chagrined smile. "Cover."

She shook her head, feeling nauseous. "All this time, all this time I thought I was responsible for your death."

Jim sat beside her, running his fingers through his hair. "I didn't realize that until recently. That's one of the reasons I'm here. Why I asked to give you the new assignment."

"What have you been doing all this time? Why did we all need to think you were dead?" Hannah asked.

"Smoking out the straggling members of Kyle's group. There were several higher up in the food chain still around. When Kyle escaped, I knew I had to see to your safety."

"Again."

Jim nodded, his face held in flat, tight lines.

She turned to Jernigan. "Still no word?"

The Marshal shook his head.

She returned her attention to Jim. "Why are you off your cover now?"

"All are either eradicated or neutralized." Jim sighed. "I've taken a semi-leave of absence. I came to see you."

Hannah turned away from the men. She secured the robe around her waist with a tight twist to the ties. "Is that the leave of absence you were talking about? How is that going to hurt your career?"

Ward stepped forward and touched her shoulder. "Actually, I was the one taking a leave of absence."

"Or maybe a permanent leave," Jernigan said.

Hannah spun around, her bare feet screeching on the linoleum. "What are you all talking about?"

"I'm coming with you on your new assignment."

Ward spoke low, and it took a moment for his words to sink in. She rubbed at her temples. A pounding headache formed behind her eyes. But a hot swell of emotion filled her heart. She wouldn't have to leave Ward behind. He wanted to come with her. She hadn't ruined everything by not being able to return the words she knew he wanted to hear.

Ward said leave of absence.

Jernigan said permanent.

The marshal had always played it straight with her. His honesty was always something she could count on. She knew he spoke the truth now.

If Ward left with her, he wouldn't be welcome at the Bureau when he came back.

She wouldn't let another person sacrifice for her. Jim had, or so she'd thought, and the responsibility for what she had presumed until now was his death had nearly killed her with guilt.

The Bureau was all Ward had ever wanted. What he lived for. What he was.

As they'd sat trapped in the elevator, she felt his need to right the wrongs of the world. Then she just thought it was through his security job, now she understood it went deeper, working with the government. Finding the types of criminals who killed his parents. She couldn't take that away from him.

For her.

With a shrug, she shook his hand from her shoulder. She steeled her features and turned to face him.

"No, Ward. I don't want you to come with me."

"Hannah, it's what I want to do."

"But I don't want you to make the sacrifice."

He shook his head and smiled, his voice low. "Being with you would never be a sacrifice."

Her eyes met his. She had to make him leave. "You don't understand. I don't want you in my new life."

The smile left his face, and his hands fell to his side. His gaze searched hers.

He took a few steps back, then turned his back to her. With a curt nod to the other men, he moved toward his room. "I'm packing up."

She tamped down every emotion, every desperate urge to call him back. *Be strong.* She would not let another person forfeit his life for hers.

She had to get out of there. She had to be strong, but she didn't have to hear Ward pack and see him drive off.

Hannah turned to the other men. "I'm going out to the boat dock for a while."

The gravel poked into her bare feet, and the twigs snagged at the terry cloth loops of her robe, but she wasn't going to the room next door to Ward's to change her clothes.

Lifting the edges of the robe, she increased her speed, nearly running to the boat pier. Taking deep breaths, she gathered a few rocks and stepped onto the floating dock.

Rolling the loose ends of her robe beneath her thighs, she plunged her legs into the water. The night air was beginning to cool. Out here away from the city lights, the stars overhead burned so bright.

She'd spent a lot of time looking up at the stars as a

little girl. Even during the darkest times, they'd reminded her of the big world waiting out there for her to explore. Tonight they just made her think of how little she really was. How unsolvable her problems were. How Ward, when he left in a few minutes, would be taking something of her with him.

Hannah grabbed a rock and let it slip from her fingers into the water. She didn't even have the urge to hurl the stone. She'd just let it sink.

When had she given him her love?

She'd sensed her danger at Protter and Lane. And not the kind of danger to her life, but to her heart.

The boat dock shifted, and footsteps creaked on the wood.

Jim crouched down beside her. "Mind if I join you?"

She shrugged her shoulders.

"I know it was hard for you, but you did the right thing sending him off."

She picked up a rock and tossed it onto the water. Four skips. "I always do the right thing now."

Jim picked up a rock and skipped it. Or tried.

Hannah laughed, clutching to the humor to avoid hearing Ward open the trunk of his car.

"You taught me to skip rocks. Remember?" she asked.

"I think I'm a little rusty."

The moon shone brightly overhead, illuminating his face. "You know, you always seemed so much older four years ago. But really, you're not much older than I am. Must be all that hard living."

He turned and looked at her. The corners of his eyes crinkled. "Same old Sarah."

She'd meant to put on some clothes and run a comb through her hair, but then the pull of Jim's familiar voice had drawn her into the front room. He smoothed the hair from her face. She must look a mess.

Jim held a strand. "Not everything's the same. What do you call this hair color?"

"The bottle says Scarlet Blaze."

He dropped her hair. "Unusual for you to pick something that would draw a lot of attention to yourself. Some might even call that color sexy."

The rock slipped from her hand, sinking into the water below with a thunk. "Until you said anything, I hadn't even realized…"

"We'll start on your new identity tomorrow. I think you'll like Atlanta."

She looked out onto the water. "Great, another humid place."

"We won't be able to keep you in computers. That's just too hot. We have a series of jobs. You can take your pick. We'll give you the training to—"

"Jim, I'm not going."

"If you feel that strongly about Atlanta, we could try someplace else."

Mama duck paddled by in the distance, her babies swimming in circles about her. "No, not Atlanta, not anywhere else. I'm not leaving here."

"Sarah, what are you talking about? You're compromised. You can't stay here."

With slow movements, Jim stood beside her. "I think you've lost it. Stress from tonight. We'll discuss this in the morning when you're rational."

She reached for his shirtsleeve. "Jim, I can't keep running. I *won't* keep running. I'm ready to stop." Even if she couldn't have a future with Ward, she was ready to face a future with no fear. Her fearful days were over.

"So we wait here for him to find you and kill you? Not an option."

"No, we trap him."

"How will we find him? We don't even know where he is."

"But you will."

"How?"

She swallowed hard. The blood raced through her body, her senses on fire. She felt empowered. The only time her nerves flamed with such charge was when she made love to Ward.

"He'll come to us if you use me as bait."

17

"SARAH." JIM SHOOK HIS HEAD. "Hannah, you don't know what you're saying."

Hannah smiled. "Actually, Jim, this feels so right, I know it's not wrong."

Hannah began making her way back to the safe house. Ward's and Jernigan's voices drifted to the dock. She couldn't make out the words, but the sounds rang harsh and angry in the air.

"If this is because of him…"

She stopped walking, and caught Jim's arm. "No, it's not him. Something's been changing inside me for a while. You noticed it yourself."

His expression remained skeptical. He clearly did not believe her.

Pushing her hand into her mass of tangled curls, she shook her hair at him. "Scarlet Blaze. You tell me that's not the color a woman picks out to get a little sex appeal."

Jim's lips twisted in a smile.

"Ward may have sped things up, but eventually I would have been in this same place without him."

"You're risking your life."

"But Jim, don't you see? I wasn't really living. These last few weeks have been magical."

"Is the magic worth your life?"

"I can't go back to the day-to-day existence, with no color in my life."

His gaze dropped. "At least you *had* it."

"And I plan to keep it."

"Do you love him?"

Hannah looked toward the water. Mama duck nipped at the ducks and quacked. "I, uh…"

"That's not the correct answer." Jim angled his head toward Ward. "The man over there loves you. He was willing to kiss off his career, so you'd better be sure about this. Otherwise take the reassignment, and be the bait next time. If there is a next time."

She smiled. "Let me try that again. Yes, I do." Overcome with a sense of well-being, she stood steadfast, refusing to bow down to any uncertainties. How had the words slipped out just now?

"Maybe you should say it to him."

"It's a lot easier just telling it to you."

Jim laughed.

She glanced at Ward. He tossed a large duffel bag of clothes into the backseat. He held his body stiff, his anger apparent. Her heart began to fold.

She winced. "He's pretty mad."

"I think he'll get over it."

Wicked thoughts entered her mind. "Yeah, I think he will."

Jim reached for her hand, stopping her from walking

to Ward. "One last chance to back out. You sure about this?"

She glanced one last time at the lake. Mama duck had all her babies lined safely in a row. They paddled peacefully across the lake. "Yes. I *need* this. I need to really start over."

To her surprise, Jim smiled. "Hot damn. Let's go trap ourselves a convict."

With a whoop, Hannah took off. The twigs and rocks didn't bother her feet as she soared toward Ward.

He looked up as she approached, his body still tense. How was she going to handle this one?

The two marshals were helping him organize his groceries on the floorboard. She couldn't speak her heart with them hanging around. Her decision made, if she never saw another marshal again it would be more than fine.

"Eric, Jernigan. Will you excuse us, please?"

Her heartbeat jumped as she waited for the two men to go. *This was it.* She had to convince Ward of this plan, to stay with her, or she might as well go to Atlanta. She didn't even know if he would listen to her.

The front door closed behind the three men, and she turned to face Ward.

The warmth in his eyes had chilled to a cold, flinty emerald.

She took a deep breath. "Ward—"

"Move away from the car."

He took a step to the driver's side, but she blocked his way. "No, Ward, wait. I need to talk to you."

"You said all you needed to say in there."

Ward reached for the door handle, but she grabbed his hand. He shook her fingers off in one deft movement.

"Five minutes. Give me five minutes and I'll never ask anything from you again."

With a nod from Ward, she had her cue.

Where to begin? How to begin? "The feelings I have for you are nothing I've ever experienced before. I never want what we have to end."

His eyes met hers. The rigid stance of his body didn't yield, but a bit of the coldness in his eyes chipped away. "Why'd you tell me to go?"

"I was trying to protect you."

Ward shook his head. "I don't need you to make my decisions for me."

"I guess I was trying to protect myself, too. The longer I'm with you, the harder it will be to say goodbye."

Ward turned his head, his eyes narrowing as he looked into the darkness of the night. "We don't have to say goodbye. I can leave the Bu—"

"No!"

Her raised voice drew his attention back to her.

"I know how much the FBI means to you. I could never ask you to give it up. Give it up for me."

He leaned against the car. "I don't know. There are a lot of advantages to not being shot at. I could work security. We already know I have a knack for it."

"Don't make light of it, Ward. You'd hate every minute."

His gaze pierced hers, sending shock waves through her body. If she'd had any doubt about her plan of action before, it all faded now. "When you leave, I'd like to go with you. I messed up before, I didn't ask. When you leave, may I go with you?"

Tightness constricted her throat, and she had a hard time swallowing. With a rush of love for this man, she flung herself into his arms. Her joy was complete when he gathered her closer.

She buried her face in his neck, and breathed in the musky male warmth of him. "I'd say yes, but I don't plan on leaving."

He thrust her away. "What?"

"I plan to draw Kyle out. Bring him to me so you can recapture him."

His arms folded in front of his chest. "No, I can't let you do this."

"I don't need you to make my decisions for *me*."

"Hannah, do you realize what you're saying? You could be throwing away any chance you have with this idea. What did Jim say?"

"He loved it."

Ward shook his head.

"If I don't do this, I will never have a future. It will always be the same. Me on the run. I can't...no, I *won't* do it anymore. I'm ending the running now."

The tension in his shoulders lessened. *She almost had him.* Hannah reached for his hands. His fingers tightened around hers, and she closed her eyes.

"If you do this, he may kill you in the process." Ward's voice held warning.

Her resolution didn't waver. "At least I tried. Then at least I fought him. I didn't before, and I've regretted it ever since. I fled."

"Hannah, you couldn't. Fleeing was your only choice."

"It's not my only choice now. Now I choose to fight."

She extended her hand toward him. "Will you join me?"

Indefinable emotions chased across his face. With a tight nod, he reached for her hand.

Joy like no other filled her heart, and she drew him back to the safe house and up the steps.

After an affirmative nod from her, Jim extended the telephone.

Despite her resolve, her fingers shook as she dialed. "Mr. Protter? I just called to tell you my doctor has given me the okay to come back. I'll be in at nine Monday morning."

THE STEEL-AND-GLASS buildings of Gallem's downtown were a welcome sight. Although she missed the quiet serenity of the lake at the safe house, navigating her way through all the one-way streets of downtown heightened her excitement. She could *feel* the reckoning to come.

She pulled into the parking garage and cut the car engine.

Ward handed her a small black device. "Keep this with you at all times."

"Oh, good idea," Waverly said from the backseat. He was posing as the new security guard Ward had hired.

"What is it?" Hannah asked.

"It's a direct pager. You press this button, it alerts me immediately."

"Very cool. Does it have global positioning?"

Ward winked. "I'll find you."

Several men and women dressed in business attire passed behind Ward's car window. She saw the regret lining his face. He'd agreed to the plan, but he still wasn't happy with the execution.

She, on the other hand, itched to get started.

Ward checked his own pager. "I think we're all set. When we get into the office, act natural. Don't let anyone—"

"I know, I know. We've been through this a thousand times."

He glanced toward Waverly and his voice lowered. "I just want to keep you safe."

Her heart swelled again with the strong emotions she had for him. "I know."

Waverly turned away, his disgust obvious.

Hannah swallowed her laugh. She almost felt like the mom whose child was embarrassed at parental displays of affection.

Ward gave her a wink. "This is it. You go into the office first. I'll follow shortly."

"And thank you, Eric."

"I'll always be around," he said.

She leaned to the backseat and kissed the young marshal's cheek, smiling as a blush tinged the tips of his ears.

She hooked the plastic black box onto her waistband next to her old pager. "This could become a fashion statement."

Ward gave her a tight smile. With a wink, she left the car, each step closer to the elevator quickening her excitement.

Tapping her toe as she waited for the lift, relief raced through her when the *other* elevator dinged its arrival. She wasn't quite up to riding in the elevator she and Ward had been trapped in. Nearly made love in.

Someone bumped into her stepping into the elevator with her, but the usual breathlessness of claustrophobia didn't assail her. When someone's purse accidentally brushed her leg, she didn't tense.

She smiled as she exited and made her way onto her floor. Her steps faltered as she walked to her office. A crowd of people stood outside her door. A Welcome Back poster hung suspended from the transom.

"There she is." Dinah rushed forward and gave her a hug.

"We're so glad you're back," Harry from accounting said.

"You look pretty good," Lisa from human resources said with a smile.

Dinah drew her to her office. "I made you a cake."

"Oh, you shouldn't have."

"After you eat it, you'll really think that."

Overwhelmed by the kindness of her coworkers, Hannah swallowed several times. Various workers at P&L sat around her office, eating Dinah's cake. She'd missed this kind of camaraderie all her life. Who knew what her future would hold? But she planned to enjoy these small pleasures in life to the hilt.

Ward showed up and introduced Waverly as Derrick Ware, a security consultant. But she knew he was really there for her protection when Ward staged the raid on the offices. She knew it was only a matter of time now.

Did it make her a bad person because she wished it would be later rather than sooner?

Her coworkers laughed and joked in her office for some time until Mr. Protter showed up. As the crowd dispersed, Dinah stayed behind.

"Hannah, I celebrated your first day back by forgetting my password."

Hannah laughed. "Just like old times. Have a seat, I'll set you right up."

"You're not going to get me sick, are you?" Dinah asked.

"I'm fully recovered. Not contagious anymore." Happy for the distraction, Hannah invited her in. "We haven't had a chance to chat since I got back."

Dinah reclined in the chair in front of Hannah's desk. "Really, these are the most uncomfortable chairs. Where did you dig these up from?"

"Maybe it's time for a change."

"Oh, and speaking of changes, what's up with you and the security guy?"

Hannah smiled.

"Oh, come on. I can tell by that grin there's something going on. Now spill. The way he hovered over you as you ate your cake."

She'd always wanted a female confidante. With Dinah, she could share all the giddy emotions boiling inside her. Albeit with a nice, rehearsed cover story.

"We started talking that day he came to deliver my laptop and some of the discs from Mr. Protter so I could keep things working from home. He found a reason to come by every day."

"Is he as good in bed as he looks?"

Heat filled her cheeks. Confidante or not, there were some details Hannah planned *not* to share.

"That blush tells it all. He's better, isn't he?"

Hannah just laughed.

"Man, some girls have all the luck." The unhappiness in Dinah's voice triggered a sadness in Hannah.

"One of your notes said you were seeing a new man. Are things not going well?"

A stricken look crossed Dinah's face, and she reached for the little stuffed animal on Hannah's desk. Her first doodad. "I've really missed you. This new guy—"

Her words cut off abruptly, and she looked out Hannah's door. Standing up, Dinah smoothed her skirt. "There's Da—uh, Mr. Protter now. I better make it look like I'm working before he fires me."

The words were meant as a joke, but they fell flat. Dinah's usual perkiness had vanished.

Hannah grasped the other woman's hand. "Join me for lunch. We'll close the office door and have a nice chat."

Dinah gave her a tight smile, and nodded. "Thanks."

THAT EVENING, at her apartment, Ward poured her a drink. "How was your first day back?"

"Great, but kind of anticlimactic at the end."

He stretched his long legs beside her on the couch. "Why's that?"

"I guess I just sort of expected something to happen today."

"Ah, a novice. We professionals at the FBI pride ourselves on our patience."

"And I have the carpet burns on my back to prove it."

Ward lifted an eyebrow. "That sounds like a challenge."

His face turned serious, "Hannah. I have something I want you to look at. These are the computer transactions that are skimming the money from deposits."

He handed her a sheaf of paper. It took only a moment to see the problem. She pointed to a series of numbers and symbols. "These aren't my codes. Someone's changed my stuff."

With a smile, Ward slapped the paper with his finger. "This is our key."

He stood, twirling her around. "We determine who changed your codes, and we have our suspect."

"No one can change my codes."

Ward rolled his eyes. "You computer geeks are all the same, no one can hack your stuff."

She poked him in the chest. "You'll pay for that geek comment."

"You solve this, and I will gladly."

A rush of sexual heat flooded her body.

He reached for her hand. "Think. Who is someone that's been in your office a lot? Someone you would trust?"

"Few people come to my office. They usually call when they can't get their e-mail."

"Think. Small visits. Someone chatty. Someone friendly."

Her heart skipped. This sounded familiar.

Dinah.

Ward smacked the papers on his hand. "Right. Of course it's Dinah."

She hadn't realized she'd said her friend's name aloud. But it made sense now. All those lost passwords. She'd had plenty of time to observe how Hannah got into the system.

"That would explain why no real activity took place while I was gone. I changed the password while at the safe house."

A sense of sadness at Dinah's betrayal made her heart tighten. She'd begun to think of Dinah as the kind of friend she'd always yearned for.

"And she's been in your office plenty of times since you got back."

Hannah nodded. "Yes, she forgot her password. She hadn't forgotten it once while I was away."

"This makes all the puzzle pieces fit nicely. I've suspected Protter for some time, but he's not a details man. He couldn't hack into your system. Dinah's been having an affair with Protter."

Yes, it explained so much. The slip of the tongue, the melancholy.

"Why would Protter want to steal from his own company? He's already so rich."

"I wondered that, too. First, never underestimate how much money one person wants. The second reason is Arvest Lane. He's taking over, pushing Protter aside. Protter basically has no more authority or decision-making power. He didn't even want me here in the Gallem office, it was Lane who hired me."

Ward kissed the top of her head. "Hannah, you're great. This is it. I'm going to secure the warrants."

"Wait. Ward, do me a favor. If Dinah's involved, promise me you'll seek a plea or something. He must be coercing her. She's not a criminal."

The smile left his face. "I only gather the evidence. I'm not the Justice Department."

"Just do what you can."

He nodded. "I will. I'll let the undercover guys downstairs know I'm leaving. Do you want me to send Jernigan to stay? On the couch."

She laughed. "No, I'll be fine."

With a wave, he left.

She checked her urge to call him back. To make him wait a little longer.

If he were right about Dinah and Mr. Protter, then his case would be over. He would be going back to Washington, D.C.

18

WARD DIDN'T GO INTO the offices of P&L the next day. Instead he drove out to the FBI's Gallem satellite office to report to his supervisor and clear the way for the next phase of the operation. Dozens of FBI agents swarmed the offices of Protter and Lane to remove files, computers and everything they thought could be used as evidence.

They also arrested Dinah and Dan Protter.

Arvest Lane would be flying into Gallem later that night and would expect a full report of what was left of the company in the morning. The talk in the hallway and around the water cooler was that Lane would probably shut the office.

Damn. That would mean she'd have to find another job, too. Of course, this time she could keep her Hannah Garrett résumé. Her telephone rang, thankfully drawing her attention away from her future, one that may not include Ward. He hadn't spoken of love or a future. And she didn't ask. But he did tell her he'd left a mysterious package for her in her apartment.

He'd basically moved in with her after they left the safe house. A marshal still stayed in the parking lot of her complex, but as Ward was with her, Waverly didn't have to sleep on her couch. Not that she'd seen him much. His mother had been sick, and he'd left for a quick visit.

It felt strange living with a man again, and all the weird stuff that came with him. Her little apartment felt delightfully cramped right now. She saw something large and unexpected leaning against the wall. This had to be her mysterious present. Ward keyed in just as she'd yanked off the sheet surrounding it. "Ward, do you want to explain why this is here?"

He poked his head around the corner to see her pointing to the nude that had been in the safe house.

"I think we should take the painting."

"I am not having that thing in my living room."

He stepped up behind her, wrapping his arms about her waist. "Remember how I promised I was going to make you look like the woman in the painting?"

She closed her eyes as he nuzzled her neck. Already turning to deepen the embrace, she wrapped her arms around him. "Yeah, I think I told you it was never going to happen."

He winked. "What can I say? I got you eating out of my hand."

She swatted him with a stack of newspapers.

He grabbed her up in his arms. "You know I'm your pleasure slave."

Hannah laughed. He lowered his head to kiss her as his pager vibrated.

With a groan, he pulled away. "Why now?" He pressed a few buttons on the pager. "Looks like they

need me to come into the satellite office. Do you want
to come with me?"

"No, I have to throw this big painting away."

His face looked pained. But he winked, grabbing his
jacket as he left.

As he closed the door behind him, Hannah reached
for the last stack of newspapers ready to take them to
the recycling box.

She grabbed at the front page, her fingertips dark
from the newsprint. Maybe she could fingerprint Ward
later. That would be a switch for her lawman. Her
lawman. She liked the sound of that.

The muscles propping her smile slackened.

She shook out a newspaper and a picture floated to
the ground. Actually it was a picture torn in two. She
flipped the pieces together and fitted them together.
She and Kyle. Ripped down the middle.

The glass slipped from her hand to the floor, shat-
tering.

The newspaper fluttered to the tile as she raced to
the door. Hannah threw the dead bolt, the click resound-
ing safely throughout the front room.

She turned and rested her back against the door. The
hard wood cut into her shoulders, but she didn't care.

This was the reason Kyle hadn't struck yet. He'd
been waiting for her to get comfortable. Be alone.
Today.

The black walls of her apartment seemed to
expand, emphasizing the truth. She was truly alone
for the first time.

She raced to the phone to call Ward. Picking up the

receiver, she heard nothing but dark dead silence. She felt for the pager at her waist.

"Looking for this?"

The cold steel of the voice made her whip her head around. Kyle Barton. He stood framed in her bedroom doorway, calm, smiling, and holding her pager. The ice of his blue eyes pierced her. Prison had hardened the lines of his face, and his arms bulged with muscles. He looked scarier and stronger than ever before. Even with her karate training, she doubted she could overpower him.

He clicked the pager with an immaculate thumbnail. She lunged for it.

"*Tsk. Tsk.* Is this what you're wanting to do? Alert your boyfriend?"

He moved into the living room. With slow, deliberate movements, Kyle then pressed the button. "This should bring him right along. Would you care to join me on the couch while we await his arrival?"

How dare he come into her home? Touch her things. "I'm not just going to wait here calmly for you to kill me."

Kyle smiled. "Ah, Sarah, I wouldn't want it any other way."

Hearing her name on his lips sent a ripple of fear down her back. She hated him saying her name. The spooky way he said it still haunted her dreams. The sight of him sitting on her couch filled her with a red-hot rage.

She took a deep breath. "My name is Hannah."

She whirled on her heel and raced for her bedside table, where she hid her gun. She felt with her palm, but nothing. She hadn't packed this room yet. Her Taser was nowhere near. Where could her gun be?

A laugh sounded behind her.

She turned to see her weapon dangling from his index finger.

"Waverly was very thorough, wasn't he? I still know all your secrets, Sarah. You can never hide from me."

"Waverly?"

"Didn't your boyfriend tell you? He and Jernigan got rid of him as soon as they figured out Waverly's past job as a prison guard."

Hannah sidled her way toward the window. Jernigan was outside in the parking lot; he'd see a signal.

Kyle smiled. "I wouldn't bother. Jernigan's not going to wake up for a long time. If at all."

She sucked in a gasp. It was Jim all over again.

The lock turning in the cylinder alerted her to Ward's arrival. Quick. He must not have driven too far from the apartment when Kyle paged him.

"Ah, looks like our final guest has arrived. Shall we begin?"

Fear for Ward propelled her into action. She charged her adversary as she screamed. "Get out, Ward. It's a trap."

Kyle caught her arm. His superior strength pinned her to his side. He pulled her to the front room, his gun aimed forward.

Ward's face was a mask of calm, cold anger. His gun pointed at Kyle's heart.

Hannah's missing direct pager lay on the floor. Kyle kicked it toward Ward. "Waverly said this little device would come in handy. It brought you right to me."

Ward's eyes narrowed.

"We seem to be in a standoff. My gun is pointed at you. Your gun is pointed at me."

Hannah lowered her eyes and leaned toward Kyle. Cool purpose and resolve filled her. She would not be afraid. "He means nothing to me. Just my last guard. Tie him up and let's go."

Kyle shook his head. "No, he means more to you than that. Where do you think I should shoot him? His head? That's a quick death." Kyle lowered the gun. "Or his stomach. Painful and slow."

Hannah sucked in her breath.

Kyle's grip tightened around her arm. "Painful and slow sounds good to me."

Ward lifted his chin. "Give it your best shot."

Kyle cocked his head. "No, I don't think so. How about if I let you live, but I do something like this?"

Kyle turned the gun, pressing the cold tip of the barrel to her temple.

Hannah stifled a whimper. She would never let him see her give in to the fear.

"You're not going to do that, Barton. She was to be your wife."

"But that can never be now. You've defiled her."

Kyle turned the gun toward Ward. "On second thought, I might prefer to kill you inst—"

Ward lunged for Kyle, jamming his shoulder into Kyle's stomach. With a grunt, Kyle dropped his weapon. The gun clanged against the tile, and it skidded across the floor, stopping at her feet. Hannah grabbed it.

The two men struggled for Ward's gun. Kyle's foot sent

her lamp to the floor with a crash. Kyle groaned when Ward wedged his elbow into the other man's rib cage.

Hannah searched for a weapon, something big to hit at Kyle's back. A shot reverberated through the front room. Hannah screamed.

Ward fell to the floor.

Kyle rolled to his feet. With a laugh he kicked Ward to his stomach. "See your protector now, Sarah?"

Hannah raised her gun, pointing it squarely at Kyle's chest. "Don't move."

Kyle smiled.

She gestured with the gun. "Move to the wall. Now."

"You can never get away from me. Why do you even try?"

Hannah spotted Ward's jacket by the front door. His cell phone would be inside. She walked carefully between the maze of boxes in the front room, her gun still pointed at Kyle. If she could get to the phone, she could call the police.

She glanced down at her love on the floor. Ward didn't move. A smear of blood dripped down her wall.

A flash of blond hair drew her attention away from Ward. Her eyes narrowed as she faced Kyle. "Stay back."

Her former lover took a step. "Now, Sarah, we both know you could never shoot me."

"I said stay against the wall."

Kyle stepped again toward her, his arms outstretched.

"Don't move again."

His laugh reverberated much the way his gunshot had a few minutes earlier. He took another step. And another.

Her finger pulled the trigger.

Disbelief passed over Kyle's face as he crumpled to the floor.

Tucking the gun in her waistband, Hannah rushed toward Ward. Rolling him to his back, she pulled his head into her lap. "Please don't die. Please be alive."

"I won't die if you'd just give me some air." His voice sounded muffled, but not weak. "Although it doesn't seem like a bad way to go, you're smothering me with your chest."

Sweet tears of relief fell as he pulled away. "I love you, Ward. I love you."

"I love you, too."

The distant sound of sirens eased her anxiety. "Ward, the police are coming. Someone must have called them about the gunshots."

"No, I called before I came. I knew you wouldn't page me unless it was important."

A SWAT police officer charged through the door a few moments later. "Toss the gun this way, lady."

With slow movements, she pulled the gun from her waistband. "He's hurt. Please call for an ambulance."

"You two okay? An FBI agent called to say there was trouble here."

She hugged Ward close. "Yes, we're all right."

KYLE HAD DIED on the way to the hospital.

Five hours later, Hannah helped ease Ward into a bed at a hotel. She didn't want to go back to her apartment. She pulled the covers over Ward, then headed for the second double bed. The gunshot wound to his torso, although very uncomfortable, was only superficial. The knock to his skull as he fell was what had caused his unconsciousness. Much to his chagrin. Her big, strong agent.

But she felt good. She felt free.

She also felt cold. She pulled the sheets back and snuggled under the covers.

"Come here," he said, his voice gruff. He'd been grouchy since leaving the hospital, not wanting to take much of his pain medication. She was ready to sleep away the memory of this day.

"You come here," she told him.

"I'm the one who's injured."

With a dramatic heavy sigh, she walked to him. "Yes?"

"I want to make love to my future wife."

She looked over at him. "I thought you were injured."

"I'm not dead. Besides you can nurse me back to health with your loving."

With a laugh, she joined him on the bed. This was a nursing job she would relish. Ward reached for the switch on the lamp.

Hannah stopped his hand. "Leave the light on."

With these women, being single never means being alone

The Single Life
by Liz Wood

HARLEQUIN

N℮xt

HN39

Available April 2006
TheNextNovel.com